WANTED: A
ROOMMATE
WHO ISN'T
Evil

JENNIFER
KROPF

WANTED: A ROOMMATE WHO ISN'T EVIL

This is obviously a work of fiction. If you believe this is a *true* story about fae, magic pumpkins, and enchanted blossom bracelets, then I can't help you. (And chances are no one can.)

Unless…

Unless maybe—just *maybe*—you believe because you have a little magic inside you, and you can't help it. Maybe every fairy you read about was always real for you growing up, and every floating milkweed floss was a fairy in disguise coming to say hello, and every falling helicopter seed was actually a dancing sugar plum fairy twirling to a song ordinary humans couldn't hear…

I dig that.

ISBN Ebook: 978-1-990555-38-1
ISBN Paperback: 978-1-990555-39-8
ISBN Hardcover: 978-1-990555-40-4

DEDICATION

For all the broken heroes living among us.

CHAPTER
BEFORE WE BEGIN...

0

Violet Miller and the Week After She Declared War

One could learn a lot from simply watching people. Violet eyed Lily standing by the exit of Fae Café in her police uniform. The officer's sleeves were rolled up, and her arms were folded. She leaned against the door, ready to leave for work, putting on a show of being annoyed that she had to stand through Shayne's fashion show before she could leave. Yes, she seemed very impatient.

Seemed impatient.

Yet every time Shayne came strutting from the staircase flaunting a new outfit that would make the she-humans' hearts melt on his upcoming vacation, Violet spotted a subtle quirk in the corner of Lily's mouth. It was the truest sign of a person doing everything in their power to *not* smile. No one else would have noticed it. No one else was looking closely enough.

Violet smirked to herself and took a sip of her hot mocha as she jotted a quick note in her journal. She wasn't exactly an inconspicuous spy, but she'd learned to write things down that she noticed throughout her day. The habit was quickly becoming her trademark, something Shayne had made fun of her for in the beginning. But Violet didn't care. Besides, no one could guess when their memories might get swiped away in the blink of an eye—especially when keeping company with fairies. It was better to take notes for insurance.

Rain made the Toronto streets sparkle, sending heaven's tears crying their way down the windows of the café. Everything inside became cozier in the storm—the hot drinks, the crackling fireplace, the faint taste of a cool, approaching autumn in the air…

Violet stole a look at Dranian slumped in a chair by the window. The fairy's arms were folded, and his bottom lip seemed more jutted out than normal. He remained quiet as Shayne pranced around, notably uninterested in Shayne's outfits. Possibly feeling a bit moody about something.

Shayne soared from the stairwell again—in swim trunks this time. He held his arms up and flexed like he assumed everyone in the room wanted him to. Violet couldn't help it; she snorted a laugh. It brought Mor to glance up from his novel where he read by the fireplace. Mor's gaze flickered from Violet to Shayne, then back to Violet. Once more to Shayne.

"Put a shirt on before that glare off your chest blinds us all, you fool," he said.

"Don't waste your breath, Mor. You know scolding him only increases his determination to disobey," Cress muttered as he turned the page of the cookbook spread atop a bistro table. His finger dragged down each page as he read the recipes he'd put together. His new cookbook was scheduled to be published right before Christmas, but he hadn't bothered to tell anyone about it until yesterday morning. Since then, it was all he'd talked about.

Violet pursed her lips, resolving not to laugh at Shayne again. Though Mor denied it, Violet could tell her forever mate was still a little touchy about how Shayne had enchanted her. Several times. With kisses. The fact that his enchantment had saved Violet from a psychotic fox-fairy seemed to have been forgotten.

Shayne strutted the length of the café until he met Lily by the door. "What do you think about this one, ugly Human?" he asked her. He leaned forward a little too much, gazed at her a little too deeply, and when his lips tugged into that infectious smile, even Violet's heart fluttered a little.

Lily though, scowled up at him. "I'm with Mor. Put your shirt on," she said.

Shayne smiled wider. He smacked a hand against the window at her back, trapping her as he tilted his face, putting it nice and close to hers. "Is that a flush in your cheeks?" he asked.

Lily's eyes widened. She shoved Shayne back so hard he

nearly tumbled over a chair. He caught himself against the wall. "Ah. Yes. More ugly hatred. How predictable," he said, flashing Lily a tantalizing smile.

"Unreal," Lily muttered as she pushed outside to brave the rain. The door slammed shut behind her and Violet watched her pull her hat on as she walked. Lily got drenched almost instantly in the downpour.

"Yes, that's right! Go walk through the cold rain and get sick, Human!" Shayne shouted after her. "I hardly care if you get the shivers, or the sniffles, or..." He brushed nonexistent dust off his bare shoulders. He seemed to forget his thought and went to steal a quick glance out the window, taking a particular interest in the dark storm clouds.

"Queensbane, Shayne," Mor said as he leapt off his chair. He looked around.

"It's by the door," Shayne told him in a voice that was slightly *too* uncaring for someone who didn't actually care.

Violet didn't know what Mor was looking for until his gaze locked onto a yellow umbrella resting on the hook by the window. He grabbed it and disappeared into the air.

Outside, Violet saw him materialize beside Lily and open the umbrella. He returned to the café in the blink of an eye and headed straight back to his comfy chair, patting wet drops off his shoulders and shaking out his hair.

Shayne stepped to the door and spied out in the direction Lily went. "You all saw that, right?" he asked. Then he looked back at the other fairies. "She went red-cheeked." A fresh smile broke across his whole face. "I think she's fallen for me."

Three deep fairy grunts lifted from around the room in disagreement.

"It makes sense." Shayne glanced down at his nails. "A human can only fake date a handsome fairy for so long before her heart starts to melt like hot butter—"

"In the name of the sky deities, Shayne, I'm trying to read," Cress piped up. His face was inches from a page in his cookbook like he'd spotted a spelling mistake and was drilling it to death with his eyes. Mor smirked from the fireplace.

Shayne sighed and skipped off to the stairwell, seeming ready for his next outfit. "And just so we're clear—you all know I *let* her shove me like that, right? I'm thrice as strong as that thin, inky-armed human." He paused by the stair entrance and tapped his chin. "Though, brute strength aside, you have to admit, it feels like she's hiding something these days, right?"

No one objected this time, and Violet looked around at the fairies in surprise.

Her pen knocked lightly against her notebook as she waited for someone to tell Shayne he was being ridiculous. That he shouldn't accuse Lily of keeping secrets. But to Violet's right, Mor lifted his novel back to where it belonged. Cress flipped another page of his cookbook, and Dranian hardly moved a muscle from where he sat pouting by the window.

Either none of them had heard Shayne's claim, or none of them could deny his theory.

Violet flipped back a few pages in her journal, wondering herself now. If there was evidence, it might have been hidden within the notes she'd taken. She chewed on the inside of her cheek, and after a moment, she scribbled in a margin: *What is the cost or worth of a single secret?*

Some would say secrets were the cause of destruction. Others might argue a secret was a necessary saviour. A secret could kill or save, depending on how it was used.

Violet's phone rang.

"Hello?" she answered, resuming her pen knocking against the table.

"Violet." Her tapping slowed as the familiarity of the voice set in.

"Fil," she greeted, setting the pen down carefully.

From the corner of her eye, she saw Mor lower his novel again. Shayne ducked his head back out of the staircase with a grin and mouthed, *"Is that the Fil we hate?"* He looked too excited.

Fil didn't speak right away, but Violet was sure she could feel his anger seeping through the phone. She imagined the fury that must have streaked his face when he'd realized the cupcake delivery that had destroyed The Sprinkled Scoop office last week had been her doing. It seemed the journalists had recovered after their sick days off, and now Fil was back in the—hopefully freshy cleaned and scrubbed—office.

"Do you have something to say?" Violet asked in response to

his silence.

Heavy breathing came through the line. When Fil finally spoke, it was in a low, threatening voice.

"This means war," he stated.

A slow, wide smile spread across Violet's mouth. She looked across the café at Shayne's diabolical grin. Then she glanced over at Mor and Cress, both of whom were folding their arms now like athletes waiting for a playoff game to begin.

And she said, "Excellent."

There are only two minor things one should demand when hunting for a roommate:

1. Applicants must be civilized. If an individual is civilized, they will have the decency to clean up after themselves, pay rent on time, and not stick their nose in their roommate's business.
2. They mustn't be evil. If an individual is evil, they will ruin everything.

That pretty much sums it up.

CHAPTER

1

Dranian Evelry and the Moment His Life was Ruined Forever

As the coolness of fall brushed in through the magical sliding doors of the human market where hefty basins of food displayed a variety of fruits, vegetables, and roots, a former fae assassin pushed his metal basket on wheels down an aisle that was much too narrow. The low hum of human chatter flitted through the indoor market. It seemed everyone from the local villages had come to purchase groceries today, and every single one of them had come in pairs.

Well, not *every* single one. Not him.

Dranian let an old forbidden curse of the North Corner of Ever slip off his tongue when his wretched arm bumped a pumpkin from its barrel. The fruit tipped off the ledge and smashed to the floor, flinging stringy and seedy bits in all directions and slapping over Dranian's new shoes. A wet clump of bright orange pumpkin vomit clawed over the ground. The fruit's shell had split into five pieces, all scattering toward other customers and making humans leap back in horror.

Dranian stared at the rebellious gourd for a moment. He had always been taught that pumpkins contained magic. He'd heard stories of them being a method of transportation in the Ever Corners, once enchanted. But it seemed this pumpkin was nothing of the magical sort since it had not caught itself before it had exploded or helped Dranian out whatsoever.

"Selfish faeborn fruit," he muttered as he dropped to clean up the stringy and seedy bits before the humans could start stepping on them and dragging the pumpkin's guts around the market on their feet. He tried to reach with both arms first, but a wave of tedious pain launched through his useless left bicep, and he winced.

"It's broken," a nearby fool stated.

A bead of warmth fell into Dranian's stomach. "My arm is *not* broken!" he snapped at the nosy human. "It was only stabbed!"

The pause that followed was both long and awkward. Dranian glanced over his shoulder to see a wide-eyed male standing there with an equally wide-eyed female beside him. The male cleared his throat. "I was talking about the pumpkin," he clarified, nodding toward the mess.

Dranian's gaze shot back to the cracked fruit on the floor as that settled in.

With a quiet growl, he hugged his useless arm to himself and began cleaning the mess with his other one, picking up a fistful of the orange mush with his bare hand. He stood, searching the market for a waste barrel, but there wasn't a single barrel in sight.

So, there he was. Standing in the exact middle of the market with his hands full of slimy strings and seeds with nowhere to put it.

He grunted as he set the mushy mound into his metal basket on wheels, careful not to stain the rest of his food and provisions. Once the worst of the orange sludge was picked up, Dranian pushed his metal basket to the human grocery servants to pay, ready to avoid the market for a while after this.

The servant at the coin table eyed Dranian's moist hands as the fairy reached for his leather coin purse and pulled out a few bills. Dranian thought to apologize for the wet, sticky fingerprints as he handed the cash over, but he kept his mouth shut, his face solemn. What was the point in speaking up to apologize when words alone could not dry the bills?

The human servant was kind enough to place the box of cereal, the jug of cold beast milk, the three ripe pears, and the small goblet of tasty looking ice cream into a bag for him. Dranian didn't dare mention to the human that he'd also run out of pasta sauce, beast meat, and, well, pasta. He'd been craving "spaghetti" for a while but trying to carry two heavy bags for the lengthy walk back to his apartment was out of the question. Having the weight of beast milk in one hand for the entire journey was enough.

He left the market with his one bag of groceries, avoiding chariots on wheels roaming the parking lot as he headed toward the path of perfectly square stepping stones that would take him home.

His phone rang. Dranian looked down at his pocket for a moment as he contemplated. Finally, he ventured out of the way of passing people and set his one bag of groceries against the wall of what appeared to be a store for small animals.

The phone was deep in his pocket, but once he managed to fish it out, he tapped the green button several times until he was sure the two-way magic was working. "Hello?" he mumbled. He glanced over at the small monsters in the shop's window; they'd rushed to the glass when they noticed he was standing there. Tiny, yippy animals with large ears. Human realm dogs.

"Are you ill?" Cress's distinct, authoritative voice came from the phone.

Dranian eyed his arm in the reflection of the animal store window. "Not at all," he said.

"Then why is Kate telling me you've decided to only come into work on weekends?" the former North Prince asked.

Dranian thought about a few things he could say. He finally settled with, "It's called *part time*. Humans do it all the time. It means I only work half as much."

One of the tiny dogs managed to climb onto the shop's window ledge inside. The creature began licking the life out of the glass, eyeing Dranian the entire time. The repulsive wetness of the pumpkin still blemished Dranian's fingers, and he imagined that tiny beast's drool being just as revolting on his skin.

"So, first Mor found another job, then Shayne took off on vacation for the next thousand years, and now you're invoking the human right of *part time*?" Cress articulated.

Dranian offered a grunt of acknowledgement in return to imply Cress had it correct.

"Why, Dranian? Why must you leave me to bake all the cupcakes and tarts on my own?" Cress sounded exasperated. "Is it because it takes you nearly an hour by bus to get here from your faraway apartment? Do you need me to come get you and fly you over in the mornings so you don't have to pay the bus fee?" he offered, and Dranian's ever-solemn face scrunched a little.

"I wouldn't dare inconvenience you that way." Nor would he be caught dead flying through the human sky in Cress's arms.

Cress sighed. "I suppose I can't be upset since it was me who called dibs on Kate's apartment and suggested you find another place to live and all that. But we're going to have to hire some human stranger until Shayne gets back. And you know how I detest strangers." Cress seemed to be talking to himself now. "I suppose I could always convince Lily to quit her job at the human police station, too. It would be convenient to have her here more— *working*."

Dranian doubted Lily would go for that, but he didn't say as much.

"When is Shayne coming back anyway?" Cress asked, seeming to remember Dranian was still there.

"He claimed he would be in the kingdom of Florida for at least two months. Probably three." Dranian's gaze fell to the square stone path. He kicked a loose pebble. The dog on the other side of the window started barking like he wanted to fetch it.

Cress sighed again. "Very well. I'll give him a few faeborn months' grace before I start calling him to complain. That seems fair."

Dranian nodded.

"I'm leaving now," Cress announced. "I'm about to touch the red button."

"I shall also," Dranian agreed. He pulled the phone from his ear and began tapping the red button until it disappeared and the painting on his phone returned to the original picture of his straight face beside Shayne's wide grin. A "selfie" Shayne had insisted upon when Dranian first got his own phone.

He slid the device into his pocket, and he crouched down to meet the tiny dog in the window eye-to-eye.

The creature was a pathetic, helpless thing. But perhaps it was slightly adorable. It flipped off the windowsill, rolled over thrice, then climbed back to its feet and leapt onto the sill all over again.

Dranian reached for his one bag of groceries and stood. He bowed to the dog trapped behind the glass to bid him farewell. Then he continued on his journey home.

There was a grunting-screeching sound in the stairwell when

he reached the great castle of rooms where his apartment was. He came in by the secret code of numbers the bridge troll hiding in the bricks demanded he be given on his magical buttons—in exchange for safe passage through the doors. In the stairs, a female held a large, solid-wood chair in shaking hands, tilted up at the staircase's angle. Dranian dropped his one bag of groceries and rushed to catch the chair before it dropped. The furniture piece was a second away from escaping her clutches and taking the female all the way down the stairs with it when he got his grip.

"Oh, thank goodness," the female said, brushing a bead of sweat from her brow. "Thanks, Dranian."

Dranian glanced over, realizing it was Beth—the human who owned the entire apartment building castle. She batted her reddish lashes at him. "You totally saved me."

Dranian tried not to shake beneath the weight of the chair. He inched to adjust the wooden limbs, trying to take the brunt of it with his good arm.

"I was carrying it up to my apartment. You don't mind, do you?" Beth cast him a smile surely meant to put the taste of sweetness in the air. Her gaze flickered down to the chair in indication.

Dranian swallowed. He looked to the chair, then back at her. She was frightfully small. He could see well that if she attempted to haul a chair of such weight and size by herself again, she'd be crushed by it.

"I will deal with this for you," Dranian murmured. He inhaled deeply, counting the stairs ahead. Then he lifted, biting back his words and sounds.

By the time he got the thing to the third floor, Beth was clapping. "You're so strong!" she praised.

Dranian dragged the chair until it was right in front of her apartment door—which just happened to be right across the hall from his.

"I can take it from here!" Beth sang. "Thank you, Dranian!" She pulled out her keys.

Dranian nodded once then dug into his pocket for his own keys. He moved for his apartment, unlocked it, rushed inside, and slammed the door shut. His cry of agony came so fast, he almost released it into the hall before his door could seal it out. He grabbed hold of his injured arm and sank back against the entrance, sliding to a sitting position as his chest pumped air in and out.

"You fool," he scolded himself.

He sat there like that until he caught his breath. Then he looked around, noticing how dark the apartment was without its drapes drawn, without its lights on. With no one else in it.

He didn't realize how sleepy he was until he let himself lay back on the floor and stare up at the ceiling. There wasn't anyone around to disturb his sleep most evenings, but something inside his dreams had been stealing his energy. It had been going on for several weeks now—a thing he couldn't quite explain aloud if he might ever dare to try.

He was hearing a voice. That was the only way to describe the midnight visitor.

Dranian grunted and refused to think about *the voice*. The one that showed up, whispering his name in his deepest sleep. The one that kept trying to get him to let it into his mind, into his dreams. The one that sounded just familiar enough to drive him faeborn mad but still reminded him of a stranger.

He wasn't exactly having nightmares. It wasn't like what Shayne had been going through before he left on vacation. Dranian's encounters were a little different than that; a little deeper. A little more unusual.

And in every way, astoundingly annoying.

Dranian finally found it within him to pull himself off his apartment floor. He'd spent half the previous night standing in the kitchen, eating cereal to pass the time, refusing sleep so he didn't need to hear *the voice* any longer. His midnight choices seemed to be catching up with him now.

He tipped onto his sofa, landing face-first into the plush fabric. Before he knew it, he found slumber.

A knock on the door startled Dranian awake. He thought he'd imagined it, but when the knocking sounded again, he sprang up off the couch and went to answer.

Beth stood there, beaming. Dranian had to blink a few times to adjust his eyes to the hall lights after napping in his dark apartment. He spotted one grocery bag in Beth's grip. The bottom was damp, and something gooey was dripping from it. Beth followed his gaze to the mess.

"Oh, some idiot left this bag of groceries in the bottom of the stairwell," she explained with a roll of her eyes. "Now there's a huge puddle of melted ice cream and the whole apartment entrance stinks like old milk."

Dranian swallowed and glanced off at a nonexistent scuff on the doorframe. "How horrid of them to do such a thing," he mumbled, scratching the back of his head.

"Anyway, someone responded to your ad!" Beth exclaimed.

Dranian blinked another few times as he tried to figure out what she was talking about.

"You know, the ad you asked me to put in the paper to find you a roommate?" She reached into his apartment and knocked her knuckles off his head like he was daft. Then she laughed. "How did you already forget?"

Ah. The advertisement. The one Beth had suggested Dranian create after Dranian had informed her he could no longer afford the rent. The one he'd been forced to put in the paper when Shayne left for the kingdom of Florida instead of splitting the cost of a box of space with Dranian like he'd promised.

It would be nice to finally be able to pay the rent on time again.

Dranian stood a little straighter. "I shall meet the fellow right away and decide if he's worthy," he promised. "Where is he?"

WANTED: A ROOMMATE WHO ISN'T EVIL

"Oh, I already met him! I hope that's okay!" Beth flung a strand of her orange-red hair over her shoulder. "I knocked earlier, but you didn't answer so I thought you were out. I figured I'd just do the interview for you. In fact," she reached around and pulled a folded paper from her back pocket, "I already got him to sign the contract! He's locked in, Dranian!" She shot him a wide, conniving smile.

Dranian wondered if he should protest. He wasn't sure how he felt about bringing someone into his space he hadn't even met for a single second. But perhaps it was for the best since he would have picked the fellow apart and found a flaw with just about anyone that wasn't a wide-smiling, white-haired, barefoot assassin.

"In fact, he's ready to move in today. He's going to be here in like five minutes," Beth said, handing the contract over. Dranian unfolded the paper and scanned it. It looked like a binding law of the utmost stability. If he was the smiling type, he might have cast Beth one of gratefulness for her cunning. Now he had enough coin to pay his rent, and the fool who'd signed the contract couldn't get out of it, even if he did learn of what Dranian was or grow intimidated by Dranian's strength and magic.

"You still have to sign it to make it official. Do you want me to wait with you until he gets here?" Beth offered. "I should go over the apartment rules with him anyway."

Dranian shrugged and grabbed a pen from the end table by the door. He signed the contract in his most elegant script and folded it, sealing the brilliance away and tucking it into his own back pocket for safe keeping. He reached over to flick on the light so his new roommate wouldn't trip while he carried in all his human belongings.

"You may wait with me if you'd like," Dranian invited. He took a step back so Beth could enter. Beth smiled sweetly and walked in, taking a look around the apartment like she was seeing his place for the first time, even though she owned it and had likely seen it dozens of times over the years.

"What's the fellow's name?" Dranian asked.

"I forget. It's on the contract though," she said, opening the curtains. The apartment filled with light as Dranian pulled out the contract again. He hadn't thought to check the name before. "Don't worry, he's not a weirdo or anything. He was super nice to me, and he's actually kind of gorgeous. Now there'll be *three* good-looking redheads living on our floor." She winked to assure him she'd included him in that count. Then she laughed at herself as Dranian's gaze fell on the scribbled name at the bottom of the contract. It was written so messily that it took him a few tries to make out the letters. He could have sworn the fellow's first name was spelled: L-U-C.

There was a shuffle in the doorway, and Beth yelled, "You're here!"

But Dranian was still staring at that unbreakable, ever-binding contract. Staring at the decoded letters that spelled something that must have been incorrect. His faeborn eyes were reading crooked. He was sure it couldn't possibly be what he thought—

"Oh dear." A dangerously familiar, mystically alluring voice filled the apartment, sending a trail of goosebumps over Dranian's arms. The words were followed by a cold, spiteful chuckle. "I never agreed to live with a guard dog."

Dranian dragged his gaze up from the contract slowly. He beheld the fellow standing in the doorway of his apartment looking back at him. The fool's metallic-red hair, heart-shaped lips, and unsettlingly broad smile were poison in Dranian's eyes. Though the bloke stood clearly before him, Dranian was sure he was imagining it.

Dranian lowered the contract to his side, clenching it so hard it transformed into a crumpled mess in his grip. His gaze darted to the pen he'd set on the end table. Was it too late? Did he really sign the contract? Was this a nightmare; was he still asleep on the couch?

Dranian tore the crumpled paper open again to see the line where his signature was supposed to go. He bit his mouth shut to keep in a wild, faeborn curse.

No.

This had to be a dream.

That being standing in the doorway was no human roommate. He was a Shadow. A nine tailed fox. A *fairy*. And not just any fairy…

He was the very creature who'd stolen Dranian's arm.

The paper slipped from Dranian's fingers and did a slow dance as it descended to the floor, faceup, revealing his large, handwritten signature for every soul in the apartment to see.

What in the name of the sky deities had he done?

CHAPTER

2

Luc Zelsor and the Moment His Life was Ruined Forever

It all started with that proclamation in the newspaper. Luc had met with a clingy-seeming human in response to a poorly constructed message he'd spotted in the "ADVERTISEMENTS" section. The female had seemed eager to allow him to live in her settlement of three hundred rooms for rent. In fact, Luc hardly had to use his powers of persuasion on her at all.

Thankfully, he only had a single bag of belongings he needed to bring—a satchel that contained a few small treasures he'd collected while hiding among the humans. Nothing too fancy. He already gave away most of the money he'd swindled from easily fooled beings in exchange for pebbles that looked like gold. Those bills now rested in the clingy human's hands as a deposit. Apart from that, Luc only owned a spare sweater, a pair of running shoes, a few other garments he'd slid into his large coat pockets from a variety of shops. And a thin, dainty thing called a "*toothbrush*" which he loved dearly for the way it made his beautiful teeth feel.

He headed back to the park where he'd stowed his belongings in a secret bush. He could have airslipped, but the weather was breezy and perfect, and Luc decided he'd rather walk. Once he tackled the bush, he strapped his satchel over his arm and headed back to the three-hundred-room settlement to see his new home. To lay eyes upon his new "*roommate*".

He should not have been so excited to sleep in a real bed, to get running water at his bidding, to lounge upon furniture that wasn't a park bench, to meet the dumb human who was now bound by this realm's law to remain at his side, but he was.

"Oh dear," he sighed to himself, a broad, destructive grin spreading over his face. Some poor human fool was about to become his slave for the next three months. Hopefully longer.

It would be pleasant to have a servant again, the way he'd had one when he was a childling hopping around the Shadow Palace. Life had been far easier in those days when others prepared him feasts, fitted him for clothes, did the cleaning.

When Luc rounded a corner to take a shortcut between two buildings, a wail brought him to glance over his shoulder.

On the sidewalk, a childling wiped a tear from his eye. A larger male—likely the boy's father—stood over him. At first, Luc turned away and continued on his quest, uninterested. But when

WANTED: A ROOMMATE WHO ISN'T EVIL

the father's voice lifted, and a pained squeal escaped the boy, Luc found himself in the air, appearing at the father's side just in time to grab the fool's swinging arm before it might swat the blubbering childling. It wouldn't have been a hard strike—more like a frustrated jostle—but a father's strike was a strike, nonetheless.

The father's startled gaze lifted to the fox. Luc's dark, luminous eyes narrowed upon him.

"Who in the world are—"

Luc snapped the fool's nose. It happened so quickly; the father barely had a chance to inhale another breath before a thin stream of blood spurted out of his off-tilt nostrils.

"*Gah*! What's the matter with you?!" the father spat, slapping a hand over his destroyed snout.

"A lot of things," Luc said in his coolest, smoothest voice. "But mostly, I despise cruel fathers." Luc tossed the human's hand from his grip, nearly sending the father off balance. "Now, then. Be kind to your childling, you cowardly gull." He stepped in, allowing a cold wind to sweep over the father's exposed flesh. "Or I'll hunt you down, and your broken snout will be the least of your problems."

The father's face paled. He staggered back a step, then scurried around Luc to reach for the boy's hand. The two hurried off, the childling craning his little neck to look back at Luc all the while. Luc cast the boy a wink. It was a small assurance that his father would now behave, or Luc would do something about it.

It was also a lie. Luc didn't have the time or will to go hunting for this father ever again.

Luc turned to be on his way, adjusting his satchel at his shoulder. He headed between the buildings, taking a gander at the shining sun that promised this cool fall day would be warm and delightful. He smiled deliciously at that gorgeous golden medallion resting in the sky, bathing him in warmth and beauty. The sky deities had parted the clouds for him this morning. Perhaps they were working in his favour, bestowing blessings upon him for the first time in his life.

He had only one stop to make before he went to his new home. He hurried across the outskirts of the city until he came to a small orchard of trees. Browning apples dangled heavy on the branches, many already free and crushed to applesauce on the grass from whatever wildlife roamed these parts. He glided through the orchard on light feet, stopping at a great, thick trunk with a picture carved deep into its base: a circle with two triangle ears on top. A fox.

Luc dropped to a knee and grabbed a nearby branch to dig. It took him several minutes to unearth a small crate and drag it onto the grass. He batted loose soil from his hands, and he scrunched his nose when it tickled. He rushed a shaky inhale, then another, then…

The sound of his sneeze echoed through the orchard and into the sporting field beyond the shrubs. Luc froze, staring at the path, waiting to see if he'd alerted anyone and given away his special hiding spot in the orchard.

28

It was a strange thought, that he should be so concerned of humans. It wasn't as though humans were difficult to deal with. It was a mystery why he'd grown so cautious around them.

He relaxed after a few seconds went by and no other souls presented themselves. But the moment he turned back to his crate, his nose tickled again. He shook off the feeling, blinking back the moisture in his eyes. He cursed.

Could he really have developed human allergies? Had he been in the human realm that long?

He lifted his hands, eyeing the dirt as he flipped them front to back. They still looked like strong fae hands. Surely he hadn't stolen enough secrets to change anything. He hadn't bothered to take even a single secret since...

Ah, there was no point in thinking about Mor Trisencor now. It was all over, forever. Luc would be hunted down if the human news stations began picking up on his actions again. It was better to forget it all and think of a new plan.

He shook his head and chuckled at himself as he dragged the crate closer. The silver latch flicked open at his bidding, and he swung the lid wide to reveal the crate's precious contents: a few Canadian dollar bills—the last of his coin—a weathered mythology journal he'd stolen from a bookstore that told him all sorts of hilarious things about what humans thought of foxes and fae, and...

Luc pushed the bills aside and reached for a small square of parchment. He lifted it into the sunlight. It was blank, front and back, apart from a tiny dot of slightly discoloured water damage in the corner. But he stared at it, nonetheless. He stared at that corner that was once a wet spot.

He chewed on his lip in thought. Then he tossed the parchment back into the trunk, scooped out the remainder of his bills, and shoved them into his satchel.

There it was.

The sky-high, three-hundred-room settlement beckoned Luc onward as he emerged from the alley. He went straight to the thing that Beth—the clingy female—had told him was called a "*keypad*," and he jabbed the appropriate numbers to unseal the doors.

His nose wrinkled a little as he caught a whiff of sour milk when he stepped inside. There was a pleasant aroma of ice cream in the air, too, and a broad smile crossed his face. It was a sure sign of good things to come, since ice cream had a special enchantment to make everything better, always.

Luc took the stairs two at a time, then, when he was sure no one was around to see, he airslipped the rest of the way up to the third floor.

The door to apartment 3E was wide open, ready for him. He came around the corner, his nose scrunching again. There was a strange scent coming from the apartment, something that reminded him of battle. Something that—for a split second—

dragged him back to a day in the Shadow Army when he'd slain nearly a hundred North Fairies as they tried to intervene in the Shadow Army's takeover of the South Corner of Ever.

"Cursed human allergies," Luc remarked to himself. He rubbed his nose roughly as he reached the room.

A wave of the scent washed over him, and his feet came together as his flesh tightened into bumps. He was *not* imagining it.

He stood there, in the doorway, completely still. He didn't dare take a step inside until he figured out what the problem was with the air in this place.

It became clear only when Luc lifted his silver gaze and beheld the animal a mere stone's throw away, filling the apartment with the stench of northern ice, senseless loyalty, and the aura of battle stories to anyone with the ability to see wild tales tucked into small spaces. It felt like a dream of siren song—an illusion meant to torment. Luc wasn't sure how to wake himself from it.

For, standing within the confines of his new apartment was not the dumb human servant he'd signed up to enslave.

"Queensbane." Luc said it so silently, not even the perky-eared North Fairy in the living room ogling at a crisp white paper heard it.

Luc thought to leave, but he glanced over at the kitchen where the well pump rested above the sink, promising unlimited hot water whensoever he wished by the mere flick of a lever. Something within him released a silent moan as he then gazed over at the bedrooms where plush mattresses and quilts invited him to get the rest he so desired. There was even a couch.

"You're here!" It seemed Beth was also in the apartment. Luc hadn't even noticed her.

Forget the debate. He wanted hot water and a bed.

Luc stepped into the apartment. *His* apartment.

"Oh dear," he said, announcing himself to the North Fairy. A despicable laugh slipped out. "I never agreed to live with a guard dog."

Mor's guard dog.

Luc's jaw hardened; his eyes narrowed. This horrid fairy and his white-haired brother had stolen one of Luc's lives—an act so detestable and unforgiveable that it put a fresh fire in Luc's blood. His lips curled into a dangerous smile for the North Fairy to see. A tone filled the fairy's expression that told a merry story of being absolutely, positively, undeniably taken off guard.

It was truly beautiful.

Perhaps, now that Luc had the fool trapped, he would find a vile and cruel way to make him pay for all he'd done.

CHAPTER

3

Dranian Evelry and Mugs of Mayhem

It was Beth who broke the tension heating the room. Her smile went to Dranian, then to Luc, then back to Dranian again. She thought she'd done a good thing. She thought she'd saved him.

She had no idea what she'd really done.

"There's a problem with this contract," Dranian found his voice to say. He grabbed the paper from the floor and waved it at Beth. Her sweet smile dropped.

"What problem?" She took the contract and looked it over, her brows scrunching together. "I don't see a problem."

"Well… there is." Dranian's weak arm felt heavier than a moment ago. "I cannot honour it."

Beth released a strange laugh. "I mean, you can't really get out of it now. You signed it."

"You did." Luc took two more utterly invasive steps into the apartment. He had the audacity to set his bag on the sofa. After a second of looking around, he sat down and *stretched his legs* onto the coffee table. "As did I, you foolish mutt—"

"Wow, that was uncalled for—" Beth started.

"—so, it seems we're stuck in this predicament. The penalty for breaking the contract is more coin than I possess," Luc finished. He brought his arms up behind his head to relax, and Dranian felt his insides heat. Surely, Beth would not force him to honour the contract after the rude words the Shadow Fairy had spewed.

"Well," Beth said with a shrug as she handed the contract back to Dranian, "at least it's only for a few months."

Dranian blinked at her. Perhaps she was making a jest. Perhaps she wasn't really planning to force him to see this through. She could not possibly imagine the damage that could take place in three hours, let alone *three months*.

The human female shot him an apologetic smile that didn't undo her betrayal, then she turned to Luc who'd made himself comfortable in *Dranian's* apartment. She picked up the one bag of groceries dripping ice cream where she'd left it by the door, and she held it up for Luc to see.

"There are a few rules around here," she told him. "The first is: don't leave things around like whoever left all this dairy by the entrance. The second is: make sure you pay your rent on time, which can be delivered by cheque right to my room across the hall or sent via e-transfer. The third is: no loud noises—" Dranian and Luc locked eyes. There would certainly be loud noises. There would certainly be stabbing, and the breaking of bones, and the wailing of pain. "—and the last one is easy. We all want to get along here. So, be nice."

Never in a million faeborn years would Dranian *be nice.*

Luc's horrid, broad smile returned like he'd read Dranian's mind.

"All of that is written on the contract you both signed, so keep it handy and read over it a few times to remember the rules," Beth went on. "I'll pop in later to make sure you guys are all settled!"

With a skip that was far too chipper for the situation, Beth left the apartment and closed the door behind her, sealing Dranian in with the fox.

"I will break the contract. I will pay the fee, whatever it is. You will be cast out of here." Dranian wasted no time stating his intentions.

Luc brushed a fluff off his jacket, seeming more interested in his cleanliness than the threat. "Oh dear. I imagine you can't afford it if you needed a roommate so terribly. And by this binding human law, you cannot cast me out. If you wish to break the contract, you must be the one to leave." His wild eyes flickered up to Dranian, deadly and cold. "And I will absolutely find a way to get *you* to leave by choice."

Dranian growled. "That will never happen." This was *his*

apartment. This apartment had been here for him when others weren't. This apartment was the one thing he had—even if it was difficult to get groceries here from the market and the journey to Fae Café was long and tiresome. "I will repay the cruelty you showed me by stealing my arm," he promised instead. "I will call upon my brothers, and we will finish you once and for all."

Luc's face fell at the mention of Dranian's brothers. The fox hopped up off the couch, slid his hands into his pockets, and sauntered around the furniture. His expression turned serious as he looked Dranian over, taking particular interest in the arm that hung slightly limp at Dranian's side. He smiled again, like he was reliving a fond memory, and a fresh growl stirred in Dranian's throat.

"Have you always needed someone to take care of you, North Fairy?" Luc asked with a falsely sympathetic tilt of his head. He pursed his lips, then added, "Are you truly so broken?"

Dranian found his hand wrapped around the handle of his spear in his back pocket. He didn't dare draw it out, didn't dare attempt to start a fight with the powerful nine tailed fox in his condition. But his heart hammered, his arm injury burning its way through his body, through his soul.

"It seems you can't even hold your own territory by yourself," Luc mused. He flicked his hand toward Dranian. "But go. Run to your caretakers, by all means. I won't stop you if you don't think you can accomplish a single thing on your own."

Dranian's stomach dropped.

On.

Your.

Own.

Dranian's fingers slowly uncurled from his weapon. He wasn't naïve. He didn't truly think this Shadow Fairy was right…

Cress would have destroyed everything in the room at a moment like this. The Prince refused to accept comments of disrespect. Mor might have gone quiet and thought it over, but he would have come to the same conclusion—that pointed comments ought to be ignored. He would have handled it his own way, through cunning and rules.

Shayne was probably the only fairy that would have plotted revenge for no good reason.

But Dranian…

Dranian swallowed as he realized that his first instinct was, and always had been, to call upon his brothers. He would not have jumped to tear apart the fairy with his own two hands like Cress, he would not have gone to lengths to solve the problem like Mor, he would not have plotted a scandalous retaliation like Shayne.

He would have called for help. He would have let Cress handle it. He would have sat back and done whatever he was told.

And though it had never bothered him before, for the very first time, he hated himself for it.

Luc's dazzling silver eyes darted back up as if waiting for an answer to a question he never officially asked. At the look in those stormy gray eyes, it dawned on Dranian what he must do. What he would live or die trying to do.

"I will take back this apartment. I will drive you out all on my own," he promised the fox. "And once *you've* ended the contract yourself, and I am no longer bound by it, I shall kill you."

Luc's smile had no place in the conversation, but he put it back on anyway. "We'll see who drives out whom," he said in his sweet, syrupy voice.

The fox sauntered back to the couch, sat, laid back, and pulled his arms up behind his head. He closed his eyes like he didn't fear Dranian, like he couldn't possibly imagine Dranian being capable of grabbing the coffee table and using it to crush all of Luc's bones as he lay there.

Also, Luc was resting in Dranian's favourite spot on the couch. The seat beside had an uneven cushion, and Dranian despised placing his rear upon a cushion that would force him to sit at a tilt.

Dranian stifled a growl as he grabbed his rolled-up jacket off the end table. It seemed he would go to work today after all. He needed space to think. To plot.

He just needed space.

"I thought you said you didn't want to come in today. That you were invoking *part time*." Cress put his hands on his hips when Dranian walked rigidly into Fae Café where a dozen customers were scattered around tables. The air smelled of cookies with secret enchantments and freshly brewed coffee. Dranian stared at the

Prince he had spent so many years serving. Whom he had killed for. Whom he had fought for. Whom he would still die for.

There were many words trapped in Dranian's mouth. There were many words trapped in his ears, too.

"Run to your caretakers, by all means. I won't stop you if you don't think you can accomplish a single thing on your own."

Dranian turned for the hallway to hang his jacket and went to find his apron without a word. He struggled to get it on, but once he had the thing somewhat tied by the strength of one good arm, he came back around and headed for the counter to begin washing the mugs that had piled up.

He filled the basin with water from the pump, and he squeezed in a dollop of soap. The soap began to bubble like a hot cauldron.

When he looked up at Cress again, he found the North Prince with a wide smile. "You couldn't stay away, could you?" he asked. "You love this place so much."

A presumptuous fox lounging on a couch flashed through Dranian's mind before he could stop it.

"I changed my mind. I'll take the evening shift," he murmured. He dove his hands into the sudsy water and began to scrub the Fae Café mugs, wondering why he couldn't seem to spit it out to Cress that there was a dangerous nine tailed fox hiding in his dwelling. One they had all fought together. One they had hoped was gone from the human realm.

Why couldn't Dranian even tell Cress that Luc wasn't, in fact, back in the Ever Corners like they'd hoped? Why could he not at least warn Cress and Mor that the fox who had tried to kill Mor was just an hour's bus ride away?

Dranian grunted.

"If you're in a mood, I'll let you taste my new cherry-topped tarts," Cress offered. "One of those ought to do the trick." He ducked into the kitchen to go tart hunting, and Dranian sighed.

He tossed a washed mug onto the counter too hard, and the whole goblet smashed. Two females at a nearby table shrieked at the noise, and Dranian mustered as much of an apologetic look as he could with the stone-face the sky deities had given him to work with. He glanced back at the broken goblet split right down the middle—two burgundy chunks.

Even though it was mug chunks on the counter before him, Dranian saw an orange pumpkin with stringy seedy bits, broken and a mess. For a moment, he forgot his hands were resting in piping hot dishwater.

First, he'd knocked a pumpkin from its barrel. Then he'd smashed a mug atop the counter. Now, they were both just like him.

Broken.

CHAPTER

4

Luc Zelsor and the Complimentary Mix
of Shadows and Ice Cream

So, this was his destiny, then. To destroy a three-legged guard dog from the inside out and to commandeer a new home. It wasn't an impossible task. It wasn't even a difficult task, really. Luc had undone more fairy minds than he could count. It was how he knew it was rarely one great, terrible event that sent a mind into chaos. It was an accumulation of small, agonizing things, over and over, that typically drove a fae mad.

Luc smiled bitterly. He may even find it enjoyable to become the monster he was raised to be.

He tousled his beautiful rosy hair as he gazed at his reflection in the bathroom mirror. He did a quick brush of his teeth for pleasure, too, and then popped into his room to fetch his black dandelion-peppered coat.

His room.

He'd slept in all kinds of forgotten, abandoned places in his long months hiding in the human realm. He'd dozed off on park benches, fallen asleep below trees, curled up in the corners of rundown buildings. He never expected he would be the unfortunate sort to have to search for a place to sleep, but even so, it was better than the alternative.

It was better than going *back*.

Luc headed out of the apartment and down the stairs, pushing out the doors at the same time as he pushed all thoughts of the Dark Corner from his mind. The late afternoon sun hung heavily in the navy-grey sky. He looked both ways, trying to determine the direction of the ice cream shop from his new location.

It was a relief the miserable North Fairy, *Dranian*, had left. Luc needed time to let his choices settle in. He needed to truly decide if he could bear being in the presence of Mor's ally. And he needed to weigh the odds of that mumbling, scowling fool telling Mor *or* Cressica Alabastian about Luc's existence.

His hand grazed over his chest where his fox tails hid below his shirt and coat. The five he had left.

"Why can't I be rid of you, Trisencor?" he asked the wind with a huff as he slipped into it.

It took him six seconds of airslipping and following his nose to find the ice cream shop. There was no line when he caught himself gracefully on his feet, so he walked right up to the window. He knocked on it, and a teenage girl with a pinking nose slid the window open and leaned out to meet him.

"You're back again," she said. As if Luc didn't already know.

"I'll be back tomorrow, too," he promised, flashing her his dangerously magnetic smile.

She swooned a little, her cheeks flushing. "Well, today's our last day open," she said with a giggle, and Luc's smile fell. "We close every fall. We open again in the spring," she added.

Luc nearly staggered back a step.

"So, I guess this is the last time I get to serve you ice cream. You're our most dedicated customer, so your cone today will be on the house," she went on as though she hadn't just spoken words that brought Luc's entire world crumbling down. "Same flavour as yesterday? Strawberry?"

Luc nodded, but he couldn't find any pretty words or lovely thoughts to thank her with today. She disappeared into the shop, and he stood on his tiptoes to watch his ice cream being scooped.

It was a big, divine heap of glorious pink magic when she brought it back. His smile returned. She'd given him an extra scoop.

"Here you go!" the girl said. "Enjoy! We'll see you in the spring!" She waved as she handed him the ice cream cone. A second later, she slid the window closed upon all his hopes and dreams.

"Oh dear," Luc sighed. What would he do without this shop to visit every day? This shop was the reason he continued to sneak back into the downtown area he swore he'd never return to. The ice cream had been worth the risk.

He took a large bite of his strawberry treat and moaned at the taste he would miss all season until the shop's triumphant return. Closing down felt like a great crime. Had the shop been in the Ever Corners, he might have done some wicked scheming to ensure the owners weren't allowed to close their doors to him. He might have purchased the place with gold. He might have forced the owner to reveal his name and enslaved him to make ice cream forever without stopping. He might have done worse things.

But, alas, the human species were a different sort. Violent still, at times, but far less tricky, and therefore, fairy meddling often made crowds too curious.

He ran his tongue around the full brim of the cone to catch the drips as he ventured down the street, ducking around passing couples and one particularly motivated jogger. Humans tended to be chatty, he'd learned; they all walked in groups, deep in discussion, talking about boring things that didn't matter. None of them paid Luc any attention as he headed deeper into the alleys of bustling shops and down fresh sidewalks. He took a glance at the sun and mumbled a curse at it. He'd been so pleased to see it shining this morning when he thought its glow was promising a good day ahead.

It had lied. The sun was a liar.

He took a large bite of his ice cream to make himself feel better, and he swept around the bend—

He tore himself back.

Luc's shoulders pressed flat against a brick wall. He found his hands were shaking, gripping his cone, cracking the sugary shell. Pink cream dripped down his fingers. He took in a deep breath and let it out slowly.

It wasn't nerves, it was likely anger. Also, it was probably calculation. And possibly panic.

Alright, it was nerves.

His fox heart didn't settle, even when he closed his eyes and inhaled, exhaled, inhaled again. When he peeled his eyes open, he inched toward the edge of the wall, carefully peering around with just one silver eye.

Two fairies stood in the street. Fairies with elongated, pointed ears, coated in the smell of ash and darkness, with eye colours that could only be made by magic. For a split second, Luc forgot about his ice cream.

He bit down on a curse as he took off down the alley, hurrying in the opposite direction, too worried about the popping sound that would follow him to airslip. But even as he darted in and out of crowded spaces, never looking back, never stopping, he could not unsee the black pearl armour the Shadows had been wearing.

It seemed the Army had returned.

They were back for answers.

Back for *him*, certainly.

It wasn't until he was four buildings away that Luc allowed himself to slip into a store, and as he passed through the doorway he became one with the air.

He never should have gone near downtown. He had caused a mess for the Shadow Army, and now they were out for his blood. This was the first season he hadn't checked in with them at their designated meeting place. It was the first time he had refused to fulfill his role as the liaison for the Dark Queene. The first time they were allowed to abandon all concern for whose son he was.

It was the first time he'd ever truly felt he belonged to no one. And he was desperate to keep it that way.

Luc dropped onto the sidewalk in front of his new apartment building. His fingers felt wet. He glanced over to see that by some ancient fairy miracle, his ice cream was still intact. He quickly licked up all the drips as he punched the secret code into the keypad and pushed his way in through the doors. He airslipped up the stairs. He could have airslipped right back into his apartment, but he wasn't sure if the North Fairy was back. He imagined he might get stabbed if he appeared before the one-armed assassin without warning.

Luc appeared at the end of his hall and made his way to 3E with thoughts of murder on his mind.

He thought the Army would have stopped looking for him after he'd disappeared without a trace the day he exacted his revenge on Mor.

Would he truly have to kill them all? Every last fairy of his division? Is that truly what it would take?

He would do it. He would end them all, one by one, if they did not cease their search. His fox bead felt heavy and eager in his pocket.

"Oh dear," he muttered as he yanked out his key and let himself into his new home.

The North Fairy was nowhere to be found. Luc still tiptoed in, peering around every corner, eyeing every shadow and movement out the window as darkness fell upon the city. Only time would tell if Dranian had babbled of Luc's existence to Mor. Though, if Mor knew Luc was here, he would have already shown himself.

Luc's shoulders relaxed as he thought about that. He nodded to himself. No one was in this apartment. No one was waiting to spring out of the cracks and stab him clean through the heart.

No, Trisencor couldn't possibly have known yet.

It seemed his devious little comments to Dranian had worked.

CHAPTER

5

Dranian Evelry and the Thing Stuck on His Tongue

Dranian endured the whole evening shift saying almost nothing at all. The debate waged war on his mind when darkness fell upon the street, and Fae Café was lit by the table candles, the fireplace, and the dim wall torches:

Tell Cress.

Don't tell Cress.

Call Mor.

Don't you dare faeborn call Mor.

Drop a hint.

Don't be a fool…

He finally hung up his apron and escaped the café before any-one stopped him to chat. He stomped a little on his way to the bus stop, gliding beneath the lanterns' illuminations, and grumbling things beneath his breath.

If he told Cress and Mor, they could help him solve his room-mate contract problem. They could also help him kill Luc after-ward, a handful of times. And Luc was Mor's nemesis—it seemed wrong to keep Mor from knowing the truth.

But how could he run to Mor for help when Mor was in a sim-ilar situation months ago and had tried to handle things on his own first? Did Dranian even deserve Mor's help? As soon as Dranian had gotten involved in Mor's situation back then, Dranian had failed to stop bad things from happening. First, he'd failed to guard Mor's human when Mor had left her in Dranian's care at Fae Café. Then, Dranian had taken a blade through the arm and let the fox escape their trap. The fox had kidnapped Mor's human after that—all because he'd gotten away.

Maybe Mor wasn't the only option. Dranian considered what might happen if he called Shayne and forced him to return from the kingdom of Florida. Shayne would aid Dranian with his prob-lem, and perhaps Dranian wouldn't have to get Mor and Cress and their humans involved.

But Shayne had been so excited to visit the faraway kingdom. He'd purchased "flip-flops" and "tank-y tops", and he'd watched videos on the human internet about how to apply "sun-scream".

The fairy was most excited that it was acceptable to remain barefoot on the Florida beaches. Truly, the place seemed as though it was made for Shayne.

Besides, Shayne had been taking care of Dranian long enough. Dranian clenched his fists as he climbed onto the bus filled with males and females minding their own human business. He took a seat, and the vessel began to move.

He wasn't ready to go back to his apartment when the bus dropped him down the road. He gazed up toward the third floor, trying to imagine going to sleep with a deadly creature in the next bedroom. He decided he would sleep with his spear in his hand.

Dranian marched up the stairs and wrestled his keys from his pocket. He unlocked the door and peeked in. When he saw the coast was clear, he crept on his toes, silent as a moonbug. He'd barely made it through the living room when Luc stepped from the kitchen, driving a horrifyingly high-pitched squeal from Dranian's throat.

The fox stood there, studying Dranian peculiarly. A mostly eaten ice cream cone was in his grip. He brought it to his heart-shaped mouth and licked it. "You smell like coffee and that horrid North Prince," he remarked.

Dranian had a hand firmly pressed over his heart. He stood to his full height and faced Luc. "I was at work," he mumbled. "Some of us choose to work nobly, rather than steal coin from humans with fools' gold."

Luc sneered. "I took a nap. Then I went for a short, pleasant walk and purchased this." He waved his ice cream around a little. "Then I sat here and watched stories on the TV without a care in the world. I think it's clear who's winning." He took his last, large bite of ice cream, shoving the whole cone into his mouth.

Dranian grunted and marched past him into his room. He slammed the door shut and pulled out the handle of his spear. He set it beside his pillow, tore off his shirt, and climbed into bed, ready to be rid of the day's events.

He spent several seconds huffing in deep breaths to settle his faeborn heart.

To even his own surprise, he was asleep in minutes.

"I know you," the voice said. *"Let me in."*

Dranian awoke in a cold sweat, nearly flinging himself off the side of his bed. He blinked as his surroundings reminded him where he was. His faeborn heart pounded; questions haunted the tip of his brain.

She was back—the voice.

Dranian leaned forward with his elbows on his knees and rubbed his temples. If he didn't get a good night's sleep soon, he was going to lose his mind. He dropped his hands and glanced out the window at the bright moon hanging in the sky. It was probably around two or three in the morning.

On four different occasions since his childling years, dream-slippers had tried to enter his mind. He'd gotten good at tossing them out and keeping himself safe, as many fairies did over time, but this one was aggravatingly persistent.

With a sigh, he yanked away his bedsheets and headed to the door. As soon as he opened it, his ears filled with the grating sound of *chomping*. His face turned puzzled as he rounded the hall's corner, and there he spotted Luc standing in the kitchen, leaning back against the counter and eating a bowl of cereal. Loudly.

It seemed the fox had made himself at home with Dranian's bowl, and spoon, and cereal.

"Do you ever stop eating?" Dranian mumbled.

Luc pulled one arm into a shrug. "I can't sleep."

Dranian didn't ask why. Nor did he care.

Luc looked Dranian over as he shovelled another spoonful of cereal into his mouth. He raised an eyebrow, seeming to notice the sweat on Dranian's face, yet, seeming entirely uninterested in asking why it was there.

Dranian snarled a little and stomped past, fetching the box of cereal for himself. He poured a bowl, then went to add beast milk. Only a few drips came out of the bag, and Dranian cut Luc a glare. There was no backup beast milk, since Dranian had left it to rot in the stairwell yesterday. He released a heavy breath and set the bag holder back on the counter. Then he snatched a spoon to eat the cereal dry and went to the kitchen table to sit.

He chomped, just as loudly as Luc.

They ate their midnight cereal in silence, apart from their competitive fairy chomping. Dranian thought about his dream.

A moment later, Luc said, "We're out of groceries."

CHPTER

· ⟫⟫⟫⟫⟫ · ⟪⟪⟪⟪⟪⟪ ·

6

Dranian Evelry and How it all Began
in Ashi-Calla Village, Part I

She was the childling girl with no name. If she had one, she refused to tell a soul what it was. Most of the fairy folk referred to
her as "her" or "*that* girl."

Even though she had grown up in Ashi-Calla amidst the forest
fae, she was a mystery to everyone. Her long black hair seemed
just a little too luminous. Her eyes a little too bright and green.
Her skin too soft and fair. Features that made the young females
jealous and the young males intimidated. She was a girl with a
secret, supposedly the daughter of a quiet woman who never left
her house and the blacksmith who had gone missing days after she
was born. A girl with too much power at her fingertips—or so the

fairy elders claimed. A girl who should never be trusted; for when the girl locked eyes with certain villagers, they whispered later they thought they were cursed.

"A land siren," they called her. A creature that should have stayed at the bottom of the Twilight Lakes where it belonged.

Many in the village avoided her, evaded speaking to her. Most pretended she didn't exist.

Dranian was barely older than the girl, but he'd heard the rumours, and so at ten years old he kept away from her like everybody else. But like her, he remained invisible to the forest fae locals. He maintained his core duties, keeping to the edge of the village and serving the merchants at the docks to collect a few coins every month. Most evenings he swam in the crystal green lagoon to pass the time, to keep away his worries, and to avoid going home to face the father who didn't want him.

That was, until the day he witnessed the girl drowning.

Whether she'd slipped down the muddy slope into the river, or had jumped in herself to fetch a fish, he wasn't sure. But when Dranian came upon a young fairy fighting for her life against the current, he dropped his merchant buckets, shed his cloak, and dove into the silver waters, using the strength he'd built up on the docks to paddle against the rush.

She was too thin. Much too thin to battle the water herself. This was what went through Dranian's mind when he watched the girl give up her fight and slide beneath the surface, choosing to let the water take her as its victim after all. She mustn't have seen Dranian coming. She couldn't have noticed the pleading look upon his face—the scolding for giving up, the begging to hold on just one second more.

"I'm coming!" he tried to shout beneath the water, but the river muffled all sound.

He wrapped his arms around her middle and soared toward the surface, breaking through with a gasp. She was a limp doll in his arms as he paddled toward the shore, dragging her along with him. When he reached the mud, he hauled her up, leaned over her, and pressed his mouth against hers to bring her back to life—the way he had learned to do after one of his fellow merchant workers had fallen into the lake last year.

During the entire incident, he did not realize who the childling girl was. And perhaps it was by the meddling of the sky deities, for he might not have jumped into the river had he known.

It wasn't until she jolted, her body awakening and searching for air, that he pulled his mouth from hers and looked upon her face for the first time. Water spurted from her lips, and she spat it to the side as her chest pumped, as her faeborn will to live returned. When she drew her bright green gaze back and beheld him, Dranian felt an icy ribbon coil around his spine as it dawned on him who she was.

Water dripped off the ends of his hair and onto her forehead directly below. She looked more startled than anything. His arm was still wound snugly around her waist, holding her to him. He was crushing her into the mud.

He sprang back, but at least he had the decency to lift her with him to a sitting position. He tried to find an excuse to leave, but he'd never been quick with words. And also...

Perhaps he was a bit startled to find she didn't look dangerous like the forest fae claimed. Rather, the girl with no name was undoubtedly beautiful up close. It was the first time Dranian asked himself why the fairies in the village avoided her. The first time he wondered if maybe they had it all wrong.

But he was shaken from his study when a twig snapped in the forest beyond the mud shore. Dranian's gaze shot up to find a hogbeast—the largest one he'd ever laid eyes upon—inching through the woods toward them with its hungry eyes set on the girl's back. Dranian's heart skipped, his chest tightening as the beast snarled.

He was not afraid to die—he knew that much. But perhaps he was a little afraid to be eaten alive.

His hand went to his back pocket to find the half-sized spear he'd spent his last month's coin on. He tried to draw it out, but his hands shook.

"No... No, don't do this..." he whispered to himself, to his own body, to his wretched hands. His breaths turned ragged, and he cursed his condition, knowing it would only worsen. Knowing he was about to lose control of himself any second now. And so, he said to the childling girl, "Run. You should live."

Her eyes widened. It didn't seem to be in fear though—it was more like he'd said something profound.

Dranian used his last effort to press the handle of his half-spear into her palm with trembling hands so she might defend herself if the beast chased her. He kept his eyes set on the snarling hog whose snout was just feet away, whose low growl was almost close enough to feel the heat of. His thoughts tipped off the edge of a familiar cliff, leaving him blank. Leaving him useless. He began to crumple.

The girl startled him by drawing the spear to life from its handle. She stood and turned in one motion.

Dranian was almost too far gone in his fit to acknowledge that she collided with the hogbeast, shoving the tip of his spear into its throat like a hunter. The loud hog squeals filled the woods.

Dranian couldn't remember much after that, but he was vaguely aware of collapsing and feeling her sit in the mud beside him with splashed hogbeast blood up her arms. "Dream now," she soothed, dropping his spear handle into the mud. "I'll help you."

She placed a hand upon his forehead, and his body filled with tiredness. For several seconds he tried to fight it. But it was no use.

He passed out against his will, the spinning forces of his mind slowing, the chaotic torrent of noise and madness that became too much to bear, that had always ruined everything, that had made his own father think him worth nothing, meeting sudden rest.

A soft voice, a young one, entered his dream.

"Don't worry. I'm here," she said. *"You don't have to let me in. I'll just stay on the outer rim of your dream for a while to keep*

nightmares at bay. I can't say anything important from the outer rim though; the rules of dreams are immovable on that. But I'll do my best to ensure you sleep well."

Dranian was about to respond to her in his mind, to ask who she was and how she was doing such a thing, but she cut him off.

"Don't speak," she warned. *"Don't ever respond to a voice that enters your dreams. Not unless you want a stranger to take control of your slumbers. Not every dreamslipper is trustworthy—most will hurt you for their own gain if they get control."*

Her voice was remarkably soft, and he had to admit, lovely. It reminded him of delicate flowers, and a cool wind on a hot day, and warm baths in the snowy seasons. Because of this, Dranian found himself sleeping soundly for quite some time.

When he awoke, the stars were high in the sky. Moonbugs crawled along the shore, and his spear was missing from the mud beside him. He calculated the time by counting the stars and examining the night shadows.

Fifteen hours had passed.

The childling girl without a name was nowhere in sight.

Dranian spent three days searching for her. He looked for her on the forest paths, he kept an eye out for her on the village roads. He even took an extra trip to the blacksmith shop, even though rumour had it the place had been closed down for years. He wondered if he should give up trying to find her, if perhaps she had left the village.

Maybe the hogbeast had eaten her.

Dranian's stomach dropped as he considered that. He wasn't sure what he had truly seen when he was crumbling in panic—if he'd fabricated the vision of her slaying the beast. He hadn't thought to look around for traces of fairy remains when he woke up, and there was no rotting hogbeast body either.

He could not stop rubbing his head. It was as though something was inside it that shouldn't be there. An itch he could not satisfy by scratching. He'd had the strangest dream on the mud shore, and for a reason he couldn't determine, he felt like only she might have an explanation.

Also, she'd stolen his spear.

He finally came upon her at a village-wide dance in the forest hall. Dranian rarely went to such things, but he was too afraid of his father's retaliation if he did not show up this time. He'd already suffered the man's wrath for missing an entire day of work on the docks while he'd been sleeping in the mud.

Dranian was the youngest one of his seven siblings, and the only one forced to stay away from the house all day, seven days a week. The only one his family wished would just not come home at all.

The forest hall was made of spindly branches woven with braids of ivy and glass blossoms, giving off the deep aroma of freshly cut wood and spring grass. Fiddles and harps lined the far wall where musicians joined in the song at will that would only burn out at sunrise. Fairies grabbed unsuspecting partners by the hands and dragged them into the middle to dance, each couple clothed in white with tassels and lace, shifting into forms of forest animals and mimicking the long poses of tree branches to praise the favour of the sky deities on the village.

Most ignored the childling girl when she entered, but Dranian's gaze shot up from across the room like he sensed her arrival. He lowered his wooden cup of syrup water without taking a drink, watching as villagers made a wide space around the girl wherever she went. For the most part, she kept to the edge of the forest hall. She seemed uninterested in dancing.

Dranian set down his cup and rounded the table to go after her before she could escape again. She was so easily lost in the crowd with her slenderness and awareness of how the folk around her shifted. It was like she was practiced at blending in, at making people forget she was present.

Just like him.

Dranian caught her by the wrist before she could slip out of sight, before she could disappear for three more days and leave him wondering. Two fairies pushed into his path, meeting up and laughing about something together, cutting him off from the girl apart from the grip he had on her dainty wrist between them. And so, he tugged her to him. She flew right between the fairy pair and into his chest where he caught her, flexing so they would not topple over.

He was hit by the brightness of her eyes all over again when she blinked up at him. She was slightly taller than he expected, and her mouth hovered rather close to his, putting an odd flutter in his ribs. He swallowed and tried to come up with words appropriate for a situation where he'd just grabbed a female without justification and yanked her to him.

"I shall explain," he promised, but that was it. He had no actual explanation for his behaviour.

"What are they doing?" a fairy to his left asked, loudly enough to turn heads. Dranian looked over, spotting several of his father's forever-friends present. Fairies who would report him for being this close to the dangerous village girl with no name and bringing further shame to his family. Dranian's chest deflated. He thought about running away before he could feel the fear of it, before it dawned on him that he would be in trouble and he might fall into a "fit."

Two hands came against his stomach and shoved him backward.

Dranian sailed four steps away from the girl. He looked back at her in alarm, questioning why she'd thrust him so abruptly, but as soon as the gap was wide between them, the onlooking fairies lost interest, and the tightness left his chest.

Oblivious fairies swished into the space where they'd been, carrying on with their evening. Past them, Dranian could see the girl was still looking at him. Her gaze remained steady, even as the sight of her was broken up by those who passed. Dranian could not help but stare back.

She smiled.

Sky deities... His faeborn heart flipped inside of him. Her smile was amused—in a comradery sort of way. It made him want to laugh for a reason he couldn't fathom. He thought himself incapable of ever mustering such an emotion or expression, but then...

"What are you smiling at like a fool?"

Dranian's gaze snapped over to his eldest sister, Loriah. Loriah's auburn hair was braided thrice over; tiny knots woven into bigger braids, and one big braid to hold them all. Her pale green eyes took him in with suspicion. "I've never seen you smile in my faeborn life," she added, glancing over her shoulder in the direction he'd been staring.

Dranian flinched, but when he looked to where the girl with no name had been standing, he found she was gone.

Loriah released a low snarl. "Be careful, Dranian. You know we hate it when you make *scenes*," she said, looking him over in disgust. As she left him there, she muttered, "I wish you hadn't come here. You're embarrassing."

That was all the invitation Dranian needed to leave. He swallowed, attempting to let Loriah's words roll off him before they found purchase on his soul. But when he looked around and saw his elder brothers and sisters milling about, carrying pleasant conversations and laughing together, sharing a joy he was not allowed to have, he turned for the arch of branches that would take him out to the evening air, and he headed for the green lagoon.

He stomped over branches and twigs, kicking aside rocks until he got there. He wasn't angry. At least, he wasn't angry at his family. He was angry at himself.

Why had he been born as such a shameful being? Why did he lack the ability to control his illness? Why must he be the one to carry this weight on his shoulders? The sky deities had dealt him the cruellest of cards.

He tore off his shirt even before he reached the lagoon dock. The dark green, crystal waters beckoned him to come cool off.

A voice met him instead.

"The moonbugs are out tonight. You'll get eaten alive if you swim right now."

Dranian spun, his hand flashing to his back pocket where a half-spear should have been. He was startled to realize he recognized the voice. At least, his mind did, even if his ears did not.

There stood the girl with no name, her face glistening silver in the moonlight, her white dress fluttering in the nighttime breeze. His half-spear was in her hand.

Dranian's shoulders relaxed.

"You're not dangerous," he said—finding the ability to speak like he hadn't earlier. He looked her over with fresh eyes, the way he had at the river when he'd seen her features up close. "You're just a girl."

She laughed, and Dranian bit back another smile. He even chuckled—but it sounded strange coming from his mouth. He didn't know how to laugh.

"You're too trusting," she said. "The village is right about me. I am dangerous."

Dranian's smile fell.

"But not to you, Dranian Evelry. In fact, I'd like to protect you," she said.

"Protect me?" He raised a brow. "From whom?" He took an involuntary step backward.

"From all of them," she said, nodding back to the village. "I don't know how I'll do it," she admitted, lifting her hands to study them. "I'm not strong like you. I'm not big or solid or able to fight. But I'll figure that part out."

He almost laughed again. "Why do I need protecting?"

She sighed. "I've been here the whole time, Dranian," she said, speaking his name like they were old friends. "I was always there, even when no one saw me."

Dranian felt the blood drain from his face. He wasn't sure why he assumed no one would remember the things that had happened. The mocking shouts, the heartless, faeborn males and their swatting and hitting and kicking, the way the onlookers all laughed as he seized up.

"I was just a few years old then," he said from a dry throat. "It's been a while since any fool of the village has tried to raise a hand against me."

"Because you got strong," she said. "But it doesn't mean they don't want to. Just because you stay out of sight now doesn't mean one day you won't be put back into their path; and what if they or your family decides to rid the village of you?"

Dranian set his jaw. "Don't speak of my family."

A breeze came in off the lagoon, pushing the girl's black hair back off her shoulders. A second or two passed during which Dranian loathed himself. Because he knew it was obvious. And pathetic.

Pathetic that his family hated him and wanted him gone and wished he was dead.

Yet… he still loved them.

The girl's throat moved as she swallowed. "Dranian," she said in a softer voice this time. Her tone was rich with a story Dranian didn't want to hear. A story about a young boy who, even after all these years, was still waiting for his family to love him back. A boy who would be waiting forever because they never would.

A tear slipped down her fair cheek, running to her jaw and dripping off onto her dress.

Dranian could not believe his eyes, his ears, *her*. How could she cry over a story that wasn't even her own? He couldn't fathom the idea that she could relate—no one could relate. He'd never met anyone who understood what it felt like to be an outcast to an entire village with not a single exception.

Except… He had been around since the beginning, too. And it

killed his faeborn soul to realize he had watched the village avoid the girl with no name like she was diseased for all these years. Somehow it had never crossed his mind that he wasn't the only one. That maybe there were others, even beyond her and him. That reaching out to another outcast had been an option all this time on his lonely journey, and he'd never thought to do it.

Dranian turned his back to her. He felt a brush of wet warmth on his face, then cold as the wind chilled the tears he knew mimicked hers.

"Why in the faeborn Corners would you ever want to protect me?" he growled quietly.

It took her a few moments to answer. "Many want me to die. But no one has ever wanted me to live," she said.

It took several moments to muster the courage to move, but when Dranian finally turned back, he looked at her differently. He wondered why anyone had ever decided to fear her in the first place. He couldn't find a single speck of evil upon her.

She approached, extending his half-spear toward him. He didn't take it.

"What is your name?" he asked her instead. "No one seems to know."

The shadow of a smile returned to her face. "I have no name. My father left the day I was born, and my mother is mute. They never gave me one."

Dranian thought about that. Then he glanced down to the half-spear she held. "Keep it," he said. "You should learn to use it if you've decided to become my fairy guard."

"I already know how to use it," she said with a smile. "Didn't you see me kill the hogbeast?"

He blinked, then he snorted. Apparently, he hadn't been hallucinating by the river. "That was luck," he said, certain.

She laughed, and every part of his cold, steel-hard soul began to warm.

CHAPTER

7

Dranian Evelry: the Dog and the Fox

Dranian couldn't hide at work a second time. He'd taken his reasonable one day to process the horrible decision he'd made in signing Beth's contract. To accept the fact that Beth was too motivated by coin to let him get out of his binding agreement. Now that there was no going back, Dranian decided he was ready to fight.

On his own.

Dranian began the day washing his face in the bathroom. When he spotted Luc's toothbrush resting nicely in a cup by the sink, the notoriously grumpy fairy got a fabulous idea. His ever-scowl wavered, tugging up just a little as he lifted the shiny green toothbrush and carried it over to the toilet. It seemed the basin needed a good scrub.

He came out of the bathroom with his head held high, knowing that to defeat a cunning fox, he mustn't lose his cool lest he be bested by his own wavering emotions. Mastering emotions was a thing he had learned day and night in the Brotherhood of Assassins training camps. He was not as good at it as Shayne and Mor, but he was not the worst, either.

Dranian entered the kitchen and slowed his step at the sight of a lazy trail of muffin crumbs sprinkled over the kitchen counter. His gaze narrowed on the little vanilla-coloured bits, all leading across the room and into the living space. Dranian followed the horrific trail around the corner and nearly threw himself at Luc when he found the fool finishing off a muffin on the couch. A pile of crumbs was littered around him, and a heap rested on his lap. Luc shoved the rest of the muffin into his mouth. Then he glanced down at the mess on his legs.

He wiped it all off onto the floor.

"I will kill you!" Dranian growled, going for his spear handle. The buzz of his forming weapon filled the apartment.

Luc didn't even stand to face him. The fox turned himself a little in his seat, raising a brow at Dranian above his chubby, muffin-filled cheeks, and he drew a finger up to his lips to hush him with a dramatic scold upon his face. "Shhh!"

The fox spat wet muffin bits everywhere with the sound, and Dranian's fist tightened around his weapon. But his mind unwillingly filled with the contract rules regarding 'no loud noises', and he heaved in a lungful of air.

He let it out slowly as he retracted his spear and slid the handle away in one rigid movement. He could *not* be the one to break the contract.

"Where did you get that muffin?" he asked through his teeth, forcing himself to think of something other than the collection of crumbs on the rug that would bring in ants, mice, and all manner of pests. At least Luc was sitting in the middle of the couch this time, and not on Dranian's favourite cushion on the end.

"That clingy human, *Beth*, brought them over." Luc turned back toward the TV as he said it.

Dranian glanced back into the kitchen, but he saw no platter of muffins. "*Them?*"

"She brought two. I ate both," Luc stated. "You see, I was hungry because you failed to replenish your cupboards with food before accepting your new roommate."

With that, Luc scootched over and sprawled over Dranian's favourite seat, taking up every inch of the couch.

"If you're so faeborn hungry all the time, go get groceries yourself," Dranian muttered.

Luc swung back around in his seat to face him again, rolling his eyes. "I wouldn't dare go grocery shopping for you, North Fairy. I have no desire to do all the work myself and *take care of you* like your mushy gushy brothers of the North do."

Dranian opened his mouth to snap a response but couldn't think of anything to say, so he closed it again. Instead, he headed back into the kitchen and threw open cupboard after cupboard to find something else to eat for breakfast. But on his fourth and last cupboard, he realized that Luc was, in fact, correct.

Apart from the crumbs on the counter, there was no food in this kitchen.

Dranian huffed as he considered what to do next. He glanced down at his left arm where a long forever-scar covered his muscle, and he tried to imagine hauling back enough groceries for two fairies. Then he marched back out to the living room. "I'll not take care of you either," he stated. "I refuse to go fetch food by myself. I'd rather watch us both starve than—"

"Good." Luc stood so fast, Dranian nearly jumped. "We agree, then. We'll both go." The fox slid on his jacket and yanked the door open before Dranian could peep another word. It took Dranian a moment to collect his bearings, and to realize he had to find his wallet, his jacket, and his most recent grocery list.

Two enemy fairies glided down the market aisles pushing a metal basket on wheels and bickering over each and every item that was placed into it. It seemed the only food they could settle on was ice cream. After that, each fairy added whatever they wanted to their stash, not bothering to ask each other's opinion anymore.

Even though Dranian had never once crossed Mor in this market, he kept his eyes peeled for the curly-haired fairy, dreading the thought of running into him. Dranian was sure he wouldn't be able to come up with an explanation for the situation if Mor caught him anywhere near Luc Zelsor.

Luc walked ahead and rounded an aisle.

Dranian's pointed ears perked up at the sound of the fox's startled gasp. He saw Luc scramble back a step into view, his dark brown and silver eyes big and round. Dranian was sure he'd imagined it when Luc's rhythms skittered.

He pushed the metal basket ahead to see what in the human realm could have possibly startled a nine tailed fox, but the walkway around the corner was essentially uninteresting. Dranian scanned the shelves, the humans, a dog on a short leash, a few childlings running by and being chased by their parents.

When Dranian looked back at Luc, Luc was a perfect picture of calm. It was as though Dranian had imagined the whole thing.

"What did you see?" Dranian demanded, looking ahead again. He spotted no foe and nothing of the unusual or wicked sort.

"Hmm?" Luc asked. His hand traced up his chest and he fiddled with a gold necklace. "What are you talking about, North Fairy? Are you rambling on about some nonsense just to make conversation?"

Dranian stared at him, forgetting how to speak. There wasn't a single time in Dranian's faeborn life he'd *rattled on* about nonsense *just to make conversation.*

Luc released a grunt and reached for the metal basket, tugging it away and pushing it himself. "Hurry up, you fool. The ice cream will melt."

Dranian watched as Luc veered the basket far around the human holding tight to its dog's leash. A look of revulsion crossed the fox's face. He stole a look—just one, and very subtly—toward that dog as he passed by it.

Dranian knew he hadn't imagined it. He hurried to catch up, almost daring to smile. "Do you fear dogs?" he asked plainly, and Luc snorted a laugh.

"Hardly. Though one would be a fool if they weren't thoroughly repulsed by them. Don't tell me you enjoy the smell of those creatures, or the loud barking noises they make, or the way they drool on everything." He paled a little like he might vomit as he went on, carrying the conversation all by himself. "They are the most revolting creatures in the entire human realm. And these idiots," he pointed around at all the humans, "bring them into their homes and keep them as pets. I always knew humans were a less sophisticated species than us, but their love of such disgusting creatures just proves it."

It was only then that Dranian realized how much of an insult it was when Luc called him a *dog*, seeing how much the Shadow Fairy despised them.

Dranian thought about that for only a moment before he spotted spaghetti noodles. He didn't realize how eager he was until he caught himself biting his lip, imagining fresh pasta with creamy red fruit sauce and beast meat. He would be the next creature drooling on everything if he didn't get home and eat soon. He grabbed a bag of pasta—no, *two* bags—off the shelf and placed them carefully in the metal basket like they were pure spun gold.

"Let's be finished with this market," he murmured, glancing back toward the fruit barrels where a nice stack of fresh pumpkins were on display. The floor below was shiny and clean. "We'll split the cost of the food," he added.

"The cost?" Luc looked at him like he was crazy. "Do you truly expect me to pay these humans for all this? I can just airslip away with the whole cart."

"And leave me here alone to deal with the consequences?" Dranian snarled. "I think not."

Luc raised a scarlet brow. "You don't necessarily need to be left here. I'll take whatever's in this cart when I leave, North Fairy." He nodded down to the basket on wheels. "Feel free to hop in." Luc's wicked smile broadened, and Dranian glared.

"I will *not* climb into this silver basket before all these watching humans," he stated.

Luc shrugged. "Suit yourself then." He leaned forward and took hold of both sides, ready to slip away with it.

Dranian's eyes widened. He grabbed the basket to keep it with him in the market, and the fairies locked eyes, tension and magic blurring the space between them. Dranian tugged a little. Luc tugged back, squinting his gaze in concentration—a common trait of a Shadow about to vanish. All the resistance dropped from Dranian's grip as he realized he was going to get left behind.

His new shoes squeaked against the tile floor as he leapt into the cart at the last second and gripped both sides for dear life.

Luc's roaring laughter filled the market. The fox pushed the cart with Dranian inside and pointed to a human mother with her round-cheeked childling sitting at the basket's front. "Look, North Fairy. We're like them. You're just like that childling over there, only you're five times its size. How funny."

There was not enough cold in the entire human realm to tame the fire in Dranian's expression as Luc rolled the basket up to the market servants where beings went to pay. The servant eyed the fairies oddly, and though Dranian was miffed at all the humans' questioning looks, he also worried Luc would airslip without him if he got out.

He adjusted his footing to get more comfortable and looked down with a scowl when something crunched beneath his shoe. "I've crushed the carton of bird eggs!" he growled.

Luc reached past him to drag the carton out of the basket. He flipped open the lid to inspect the eggs for a moment. Then he handed them to the market servant. "I think we'll leave these here," he decided.

The servant looked at Luc in disbelief. "Are you kidding?"

Then Luc said, "They were like that when we found them."

"You just crushed these a second ago right in front of me," the servant stated in a scolding tone.

Though it went against everything Dranian stood for, he shook his head, denying it. "No. No, I did not." He bit his lips so tight, he thought they'd burst as he and the market servant engaged in a staring standoff.

Luc sighed. "Fine. You're right, Human, he did crush them. So, *he* will pay for them." Luc yanked the carton of destroyed eggs back and tossed them to Dranian still in the cart. Dranian missed the catch, and just like that, twelve eggs splattered across the market floor.

Dranian stared at them as yolk seeped into the floor cracks. He glared back at Luc. Just *once* he would like to come to the market without making a mess.

Pumpkins. Mugs. Eggs.

If only foxes were so easily broken.

Dranian was astounded they hadn't been banned from the market for eternity. He slid the pasta into the cupboard and grabbed the tin of coffee with his other hand. He reached to put the tin on the high shelf, but a searing pain burned through his arm. He choked, dropping the tin onto the counter with a *clang*.

Luc sat at the kitchen table chewing on a "popsicle stick" after having devoured a sweet ice treat. The fox had remained sitting while he'd watched Dranian put away all the cold items in the fridge first and then move on to the cupboard food. The fox's broad smile appeared, the stick hanging from his wickedly happy mouth. He seemed to make that face every time Dranian struggled.

For a moment—for one *single* moment—Dranian had been relieved to have enough food to fill his cupboards. He hadn't had this many groceries since he moved in. But... there was a reason he never put things on the high shelf. Perhaps the small joy of having so much food had made him forget that he was too shattered to put it away.

"You could help," Dranian growled toward the table.

"I'm enjoying being in the audience," Luc assured. But he stood and sauntered over with a sigh. He picked up the coffee tin, looked at it briefly, then reached to the highest shelf of all—one that Dranian would surely find too difficult to reach every morning—and he slid the tin onto it with the tips of his fingers.

Dranian stared up at the coffee in dismay.

Luc reached for the sugar next and tossed that up onto the high shelf, too. Then he went for the pasta—

"Forget it," Dranian mumbled, yanking the pasta away. "I'll do it."

Luc nodded. "As you wish, North Fairy." He wandered out of the kitchen. A minute later, Dranian heard TV sounds fill the living space.

Dranian cradled the bag of pasta as he glared in the direction the nine tailed fox had disappeared. He'd hoped Luc would tire quickly of sharing space, but it seemed Luc wasn't in a rush to leave the apartment at all. In fact, the fool seemed rather comfortable taking over Dranian's couch and TV and cereal and bowl and spoon, like it was the most natural thing in the realm. And for that, Dranian found his mood was even worse.

He slid the pasta away along with the rest of the groceries, his mind turning and brewing plots. He thought of Luc's reaction to the dog in the grocery store. And suddenly, Dranian realized the solution to his predicament had been right in front of him this whole time.

"They are the most revolting creatures in the entire human realm."

Just then, in the quaint apartment kitchen, surrounded by more groceries than could have fit in one simple bag, the fairy who hardly ever smiled, smiled just a little.

"Oh, I forgot to tell you," Dranian called into the living room with fresh vigor. "I told my brothers you were here. And do you know what they said?"

The TV went quiet. Luc didn't speak. It seemed he was waiting.

Heat tickled Dranian's tongue. But he pushed the rest of the words out, standing tall as he did. "They told me I can handle you *on my own*. They have no doubts."

Still, Luc remained quiet.

"It's not surprising. I handled *plenty* of tasks on my own in the Brotherhood…" Finally, Dranian abandoned the groceries and moved to peek out into the living space. The TV was still on, though it was muted. Luc stared at it, uncharacteristically calm and quiet.

"Didn't you hear what I said?" Dranian asked, his natural growl filling the kitchen. "I said they don't care about you—"

"I heard." Luc cut him off.

Luc sat very still for a moment. Then, he lifted the remote and the TV sound came back on. Dranian grunted and headed back into the kitchen.

CHAPTER

8

Luc Zelsor and the Bargain that Never Was

Contrary to common Dark Corner belief, being naturally cruel did not make Luc hate things easily. However, there were exactly five things he loathed with a deep, burning passion. Five things that made even his magnificent gumiho powers shudder.

The first of his hatreds he kept sealed behind a steel heart and fake smiles, never to be uttered aloud: A mountain god-turned-war fairy with too much power, too many riches, and not nearly enough intelligence to realize his only son had fled him.

The second: His mother. Who never came back. And who did not fight hard enough to keep him.

The third: Sea snail soup. An old female had made it for him once while he was on a spying task in a western village, and once was enough. He'd been more ill than ever for days afterward, and he had vowed to never eat a snail again. Some things were not meant to be consumed.

The fourth: Arrogant fairies who didn't know their place. It was simple enough. He just couldn't stand to see beings less powerful than him strutting around with their noses in the air, their tone telling stories of self-importance. His greatest source of joy was humbling fools such as those.

And the fifth...

The fifth was a new one that had only presented itself after he'd come to the human realm and accidentally stumbled into a horrifying, wide-open stable the humans called a "dog park."

Luc stared at the creature just inside the door of his new apartment, attached to a leash in Dranian's hand, its tongue hanging out the side of its face, its panting loud enough to wake a sleeping fox.

"Oh..." Luc's frown deepened. His hand slid into his pocket where his fox bead was hidden away, the gem promising beautiful, undiluted wrath to fall upon this animal should he choose to use it. "...dear," he finished.

"It's an assistance dog," Dranian stated proudly, yet still almost too quiet for to Luc to catch. The fool was always muttering in hushed tones, and Luc wished that for once he'd just speak up. "For someone with a *disability*."

Luc's gaze tore from the panting, hairy beast. He glanced at Dranian's scarred arm, then his face. He couldn't be certain, but it seemed a faint shadow of a smile was threatening the North Fairy's expression.

"Get rid of it," Luc demanded. He would not ask twice.

Dranian dropped to a knee and began to pet the animal like the two were old friends, and Luc's hand flashed up to plug his nose. The smell was more than he could bear.

"You can't make me get rid of it. Not when it's an *assistance dog*," Dranian stated. His green gaze darted up to Luc.

There it was. The fool *smiled*.

Luc dropped his hand, and his nose was instantly attacked by the wet fur smell again. "I'll kill it, then." He spun to search the living space. Where had he left his fairsabers? He vaguely recalled stuffing them behind the seat cushions of the couch for safekeeping.

"If you do…"

Luc glanced back over his shoulder where Dranian was letting the animal lick his face. Luc stifled a deep gag.

"…you'll break the contract," Dranian finished. He stood tall again, his chin slick with dog spit.

Luc's cunning mind raced over the words he'd read the first day during his interview. It had been in the fine print—something he hadn't even considered to weigh. Something about *"service dogs"* for those with… disabilities.

Luc's hand came over his mouth. He was sure nothing had ever disturbed him more. Whether it was the shock of the news—that he could not kill the varmint before him—or that this simple-seeming, failed assassin had outsmarted him, it left his thoughts in shambles and his supremacy choking.

It was the first moment he wondered if this North Fairy might really win and drive him out after all.

Dranian pulled a small ball out of his pocket. The hairy beast went wild, barking and making Luc jump. The animal began breathing even *louder*—a thing Luc didn't know was possible.

"Here, Shayne," Dranian soothed, patting the top of the dog's head.

"You named him *Shayne?*" Luc scoffed, recalling Dranian's apparent forever-friend having the same name. "That is utterly pathetic—"

"Fetch!" Dranian hurled the ball toward Luc, and Luc screamed.

The dog channelled across the living room as Luc dove over the back of the couch, landing on the cushions with a bounce. Sounds of the dog's tiny hooves over the floor filled Luc's ears. It was a sound worse than a thousand charging reindeer in war.

He peeked over the back of the couch in time to see the dog racing back to Dranian with the ball.

"Good boy," Dranian praised in his low, ever-monotone voice as he scratched the animal behind the ears.

A fresh rage swept through Luc's heart. At the dog, at the North Fairy, but mostly, at himself for allowing this to happen in the first place. But he would not hold back any longer. He would not sit by idly for the sake of warm water and a soft bed.

He rose from the couch slowly, a dark power rumbling through his bones and making the dog whine and hide behind his owner. A dog he couldn't even kill.

"I assure you, North Fairy," Luc began, his sharp eyes narrowing on the pair of mutts, "you've begun a war."

The day turned cold. Winter air threatened to arrive in an untimely manner. Luc shivered as he marched toward the ice cream shop downtown. He knew they wouldn't be open to receive him, but he wanted to check anyway. He craved pink strawberry flavour and the cool, whipped taste.

And he would have given his left arm to avoid going back to the apartment for a little longer.

But as he took step after step, killing time with his own two feet and refusing the call of the wind, he found himself in another place entirely.

He sighed to himself as he looked up at the tall building before him. "Oh dear. Why, Zelsor, why?"

The bell tower was in the same rough shape as the last time he'd seen it two months ago. All the ground-level windows Luc had smashed during his first visits had been boarded over. Nothing about the cathedral looked pleasant or inviting. He could ask himself all day why he had come. Why he would *ever* come back here.

But he knew the answer.

Because while his pride was his most precious possession, he didn't have anyone else.

"Trisencor," he greeted coldly. The disgraced Shadow Fairy had arrived nearly silently behind him.

Luc was grabbed.

In the blink of an eye, he found himself channeling upward. He didn't try to fight it.

He was dropped on the rooftop of a tall office building in a heap, the air around him turning solid, the cool breeze returning, the sounds of the city finding him once again.

Luc sighed through a pitiful laugh and rolled onto his back, looking up at a foe with skin a little darker than his, hair a little curlier than his, and an expression far more deadly.

"You must have been expecting me," Luc said. He slipped into the air just enough to stand. He appeared before Mor with his arms folded.

Mor's dark, luminous eyes were cutting.

It was to be expected. Luc had tried to kill him.

A few times.

Mor's arms were folded too, showcasing his life story in tattoos. He smelled of coffee, fresh paper, and wet ink. It seemed his little printing business with the humans was going well.

Luc cleared his throat. "Since we're bound to cross paths now—considering the circumstances—I figured I would speed up the process—"

"What are you talking about?" Mor's voice carried the same

low, guarded tone it always had.

Luc stopped speaking for just a moment. He studied the tale in Mor's expression, in his stance.

Mor stared back at him. There wasn't a hint of understanding there.

Luc scratched his head, wondering.

No way... Oh dear.

Luc almost burst out laughing, but he managed to allow only a broad smile and a half-restrained chuckle. His faeborn soul had nearly drowned in a fit of panic when Dranian had sputtered all that nonsense about having told his brothers of Luc's presence, but...

But it seemed the North Fairy hadn't told Mor anything at all. Mor's face confirmed that he had no idea Luc was even alive until this very moment.

"Well, *that's* interesting," Luc mused to himself.

"Give me one good reason why I shouldn't end your life on this rooftop, Luc," Mor said, appearing far calmer than his rhythms revealed.

What a fool.

"Yes, one reason is enough," Luc agreed, and Mor waited. So, Luc smiled broadly. "You can't. You tried a dozen times to kill me, and you failed, Trisencor. Alabastian, the legendary war hero, killed me, not you." Luc strode in until he was close enough for Mor to stab. "You cannot defeat me. You're a failure and a disloyal, marked Shadow. Remember that on the days you think you're allowed to be happy."

Mor punched him.

Luc's face swung to the side, but he caught himself before he fell. He turned back slowly, his flesh burning where Mor's knuckles had dug in. He could already feel his jaw beginning to swell. But he didn't retaliate. Truthfully, he deserved worse.

"You always run your faeborn mouth too much," Mor growled.

Luc stretched his neck back and forth as he fought the urge to hit Mor back.

"It's my specialty to speak the painful truth, even if you don't want to hear it. Speaking of which..." Luc settled his dark eyes on Mor again. "I think you know I have a problem. You must have seen our Shadow Army division roaming the streets with the season change."

"My High Court made a bargain with them. The division is no longer a concern of mine," Mor stated, glancing back in the direction of his gloomy cathedral. Likely looking for his dear Violet, concerned with Luc so close by.

"How convenient that the Army allowed you to live. Unfortunately, they will not offer the same grace to me," Luc stated.

"So then kill them, Luc. You're good at that," Mor articulated. "And stay far away from my humans and my cathedral. If I sniff you in this city again, I'll lead the Shadow division to you myself."

"Do you really believe you'll be left alone once news reaches the Shadow Palace about you? They don't care about the division's measly bargain—you know that," Luc reasoned.

Mor grunted and walked past Luc like he meant to leap from the building. It seemed the conversation was over.

Luc's eyes fell closed as he swallowed his pride. "Wait."

Mor's footsteps slowed behind him. There was no *pop* of him vanishing, but it was clear he meant to leave at any moment if Luc didn't give him an astoundingly good reason to stay.

Luc could not believe his own thoughts. His own absence of dignity.

"I can't go back there." He didn't have to specify the Dark Corner, or the Shadow Army. "I need help."

How he *hated* those words. He hated himself.

He hated that joining forces with Mor was the only idea he'd come up with. "You and I could take out the army together," he tried. "Your High Court wouldn't even have to know you were fighting alongside me. Then you'll never hear from me again."

A huff of disbelief came from Mor. "I offered you my help once. And you did the unthinkable. What makes you think I'll ever forgive you for what you did to Violet?"

Fire filled Luc's veins. He whirled around, unable to stop his tongue. "What makes you think I *want* your forgiveness? What makes you think that while I was doing those dreadful things to her, I was hoping you'd forgive me afterward? Does that make sense to you, you fool?" he spat. "I'm not here for your forgiveness, Trisencor!"

Mor pointed in Luc's face so fast, Luc hopped back a step. "And that is *exactly* why you keep ending up alone!" he shouted.

Luc waited for Mor to strike him, to stab him, to do any number of terrible things in the heated moment that even Luc knew were justified. But Mor's chest rose and fell thrice before his shoulders relaxed, and he took a step back. "Stay away from me and my High Court," he finished.

Well. That was impossible. Luc looked off at the sky so Mor might not see it on his face.

"I won't tell them I saw you, so they won't get ideas about hunting you down. But I'll only give you grace once, and it's not because I've forgotten about what you did. It's because I'm busy with other things," Mor said. "Get out of here, Luc."

With that, Mor vanished. He appeared on the sidewalk far below, and Luc didn't follow. He watched Mor cross the road to the cathedral. The enchanted doors swung open for him and slammed shut again once he was inside.

Luc rubbed his temples.

It wasn't impossible to avoid the Army division and stay hidden. It would just be a challenge.

A challenge he would have to endure every time the seasons changed and the Shadows returned for a report from him they would never get. They would send a new liaison to replace him eventually. Luc would have to avoid that fool as well. Or kill him off. Only to have the Dark Queene send another one.

It would be an endless process, constantly disrupting Luc's life. He could have fled to a faraway land like he'd originally intended, but...

He turned and glanced back down at the cathedral as a weight formed in his stomach. As much as the Shadows bargained, they couldn't be trusted to keep their word. And if the Dark Queene ever found out that a black-marked peasant-turned-army-deserter was still alive, she would force the Shadows to find a way around the bargain and brutally kill Mor. He wouldn't even see it coming.

Luc growled at himself and spun away to march across the roof.

Yes, he hated himself. More than normal today.

There were few things he cared about in this faeborn life anymore. Why did Mor Trisencor have to be one of them?

He stepped into the air, gliding past colours and potent city smells, heading back toward his apartment after all. As he slipped, he considered that the Shadow Army division must have known Luc was enemies of the Coffee Bean's High Court. Therefore, if the High Court of the Coffee Bean really had made a bargain with the division, then the last place the division would think to look for Luc was right at Dranian Evelry's side.

And that led him to recall the most baffling part of his conversation with Mor. Not only did Dranian *not* tell Mor that Luc was alive, Mor still had no idea Dranian was living with him. And Mor had just promised not to tell his allies of Luc's existence as well.

Despite the dire situation, Luc laughed. Because what was possibly the funniest part about all of this was that the High Court of the Coffee Bean—the supposed band of loyal brothers—were all keeping secrets from each other.

CHAPTER

9

Mor Trisencor and the Creepies

It was a truly remarkable fall, with bright yellows, crisp oranges, and rusty reds speckling the streets, and the smells of pumpkin and spice lingering in the air. It was cozy—a time for knit sweaters and stolen slippers and long books read by the fire.

It was a time when the human Mor cared for became the most adorable. Violet despised being cold, and the cathedral was rarely warm with its hole-punched walls and creaky boards and constant drafts. She came in daily wearing a smart business outfit of blouse and heels, yet she also layered at least one sweater over top, some-times two. And on some unusual and rare occasions, she added tall stockings up to her knees over her pants.

It was so fascinating that Mor had started secretly taking pictures of her in the mornings. He planned to make a calendar of her most preposterous outfits so she might be able to stare at them every month when he inevitably hung it up in the office.

It was all too sweet, too precious.

Far too important to have Luc arrive on his doorstep and threaten it all.

Mor marched up to the office to peek inside. Violet sat at her desk with her feet up, sipping on a steaming tea, bundled in a high-collared sweater with a blanket tossed over her lap. She was reading over the article Jase had written on the weekend.

After ensuring she was safe, Mor slid his phone from his pocket and headed down the hall as he poked buttons for a series of numbers he knew off by heart. He put the phone to his ear and waited as it rang on the other end.

"Hello?" Lily's voice filled the device.

"Can you keep an eye on Violet for the next few days when she's going to and from work? I think she's being followed," Mor said.

"What? Seriously? By whom?" Lily sounded strangely loud, like she was carrying something heavy and had the phone pinched between her shoulder and ear.

"I can't tell you. Can't you just follow her for a bit? And make sure you're subtle. I don't want her to know—"

Mor turned around to find a deadly-eyed fairy prince with a few tiny crumbs around his mouth and a splotch of flour on the shoulder of his t-shirt. Cress blinked slowly.

Lily's sigh filled Mor's ear. "I'm a bit busy at work right now, Mor. I have a lot to do—"

"I'll call you later," Mor said to Lily and hung up.

Cress folded his arms and tapped a finger against his bicep. "You know, Mor, quite recently you accused me of being easy to sneak up on. How ridiculous you must feel now."

"Did you hear that?" Mor asked, shoving his phone away.

"I heard your treachery. What fool would dare follow your human? It's an insult to your very existence as her forever mate, Mor. You should pluck the fairy's eyeballs out one by one and then crush them to jelly and make them eat—"

"Queensbane, Cress. Not in front of Kate," Mor murmured as Kate came trotting through the open cathedral doors with two trays of coffee and baked treats.

Cress scowled a little, but he obeyed. He turned to take one of the trays when Kate reached him. "I'll go bring Violet her coffee!" Kate offered. She bounded up the stairs and Mor turned back to Cress.

"How did you get past my door? I had it locked," he seemed to realize.

Cress shrugged and examined his nails. "How do you think I broke into all our foe's dwellings to unleash the fury of the North Corner?"

Mor eyed him suspiciously. "Do you have a spell-key?" he asked, and Cress looked at him doubtfully.

"Absolutely not. Those aren't real, Mor. Stop reading fairy folklore books from the library."

"Where did you get it?" Mor asked, scanning Cress's shirt, pants, shoes… There weren't many places to hide a key.

Cress rolled his turquoise eyes. "I told you I don't have one. I'm just the North Corner's greatest assassin, and I—"

"Is it in your shoe?" Mor kicked the side of Cress's heel with his toe to feel for bubbly spots or hidden spaces.

Cress jumped back a little, spilling a few drips of coffee, and Mor smiled. "Your shoe, then. That's a terrible hiding spot. I'm going to steal it from you," he promised.

Cress grunted and moved for the stairs to follow Kate. But he paused. He turned back, and he raised a brow. "Who were you just talking to Lily about? Your rhythms are all off. I haven't seen you this nervous since…" He paused to think.

"Since two months ago," Mor finished for him, his smile fading. "With Luc."

Cress came back down a step.

Mor folded his arms and kicked a clump of dust on the floor. "I told Luc I'd give him one chance to leave. That's why I wasn't going to say anything. Please don't tell the others. Queensbane, I wasn't even planning to tell you."

"Well, everyone knows you're bad at keeping secrets. It's the fox's fault for trusting you," Cress said, and Mor shot him a look. Cress released an exasperated sigh. "Fine. We won't meddle with him if he doesn't meddle with us. But don't tell Dranian the fox is back. The fool is already heated about his arm being stolen. He won't handle it well."

Mor nodded. "He'd probably go on a hunt through the night or some other absurd thing."

A cool breeze brushed through the cathedral, driving a shiver up Mor's spine. Cress headed the rest of the way up the stairs, but Mor remained, looking out the doors to the city, pondering. The topic of "secrets" put another thought into the forefront of his faeborn mind.

He slid his phone back out, looking at the call history. Looking at Lily's number.

Everyone trusted Lily to a fault. But the truth was that Shayne had been onto something before he left. It wasn't the first time the barefoot trinket thief had been right when accusing someone of hiding a big, often dangerous secret. Mor saw people's feelings in a way others didn't, but there were times when he truly wondered if Shayne actually "saw people" better.

Lily was spending long hours at work these days, yet Shayne claimed he'd once stopped in at Lily's office and she wasn't there. It hadn't seemed like a big deal at the time, but now that Mor thought it through, the human often came home smelling of unfamiliar materials. Metals instead of sweat.

Mor dragged a hand through his hair. Maybe he was reaching, fabricating a story in his own mind of something that didn't exist. He glanced up toward his office where the sounds of Cress telling Violet about the improvements to his new cookbook emerged.

Mor could be gone and back before they even realized he'd left.

Mor's feet landed on the sidewalk in a gentle whisper. Cold air nipped at his bare arms as he looked both ways. He marched up to the human police station and swung wide the door, the wind tossing his hair every which way. A few officers glanced up at him when he came in—possibly recognizing him since he'd barged in and demanded their help only months ago—but most of them seemed distracted with work.

Human criminals and victims alike lined up at various desks, waiting their turn, all crowded in, complaining and shouting and shoving. It was an absolute wildlife park, worse than a disorganized hogbeast farm. It was nearly enough to make him turn and leave again, but instead he scanned the desks for a pretty, tattooed female.

When he spotted Lily's desk, he found it vacant.

Mor weaved through the congested human bodies. He reached her desk, brows coming together as he took note of the turned-off lamp, the pushed in chair, and the absence of her coat on its hook. Papers were stacked neatly to the side, and a series of books rested by the tray of buttons for her computer. Mor slowly spun the top volume toward himself so he might read the title.

"You can't touch Baker's stuff." A voice stopped Mor before

he could flip the volume open. He slowly lifted his fingers off and turned around.

A stout officer stood there. One Mor didn't recognize, but the officer seemed to recognize Mor as he blinked up at him.

"Ah, you're Baker's friend," he said with a nod. "She's not in today. She switched shifts with me."

Mor adjusted to face the fellow fully. "Is that so." It was a question, but it was also more than that. The dawning of a story incomplete.

The radio at the officer's chest buzzed with several indecipherable words, and the officer lifted the device to murmur something back.

"Gotta go. I'll let Baker know you came by when I see her tomorrow," the officer said as he turned to leave.

"Actually," Mor glanced back at Lily's dim desk; at the strange books, "don't tell her I was here. I'll see her another time."

The officer nodded and took off without saying goodbye.

Mor stayed in the police station for another heartbeat as the noise drowned out his thoughts. Then he rubbed his temples and headed back outside.

"What are you up to, Human?" he mumbled as he left. He hopped into the wind and appeared in the cathedral a second later, noticing a fresh drip of coffee staining the emerald carpet.

As he'd expected, Cress was still going on about his cookbook upstairs.

So, Mor was keeping a large secret from Dranian.

Lily was keeping a large secret from *everyone*.

Luc had come looking for Mor like he *knew* a large secret.

Sky deities have mercy. What was going on?

10

Dranian Evelry and the Present Unravelling

Luc had been gone for hours, to Dranian's delight.

Dranian waited patiently on the couch, on his favourite cushion, watching the TV tell stories and tips on dating life for humans. Dog-Shayne rested at his side, blinking up at him with all the undivided attention of a happy servant. If only Dog-Shayne wasn't an animal.

"You're a loyal mongrel," Dranian complimented as he patted the creature on the head.

The TV story switched to a gangly looking couple who held hands, grabbed each other a lot, kissed each other too much, and kept tight in each other's spaces. Dranian found himself cringing. But what right did he have to complain about couples who put their affection on display when he'd just found far too much comfort in a dog?

He looked back at Dog-Shayne with a frown. At first, purchasing the dog had been a way to strike back at the nine tailed fox. But after sitting warmly against the creature for several hours, being gazed at with loving eyes, being licked on the cheek affectionately, and having all the attention he could ever dream of, Dranian realized he felt a small dollop of happiness for the first time in weeks.

It wasn't like Shayne himself was back. It wasn't like this mongrel could replace Shayne, even if Dranian did use his forever-friend's name. Was he being unreasonable by starting to care for a lowly human realm beast?

Perhaps he ought to find himself a special female friend like the couple in the TV show. Perhaps then he would have comfort that didn't seem so absurd to him.

Dranian found himself glancing back toward the apartment door, through which was the hall, past which was Beth's apartment. Beth was passably pretty. She'd betrayed him by not allowing him to escape his contract, but she'd also been one of the only people Dranian had dared to speak to outside of those at Fae Café this past month since Shayne had left.

Days before Shayne took off, he'd done a "quiz" on the human internet on Dranian's behalf to discover Dranian's ideal mate. As it turned out, Dranian's "type" of female had blacker hair than

Beths, brighter green eyes than Beth's, and possibly a darker personality than the bubbly, cringy human's. Even so, she wasn't *completely* awful most days.

Unfortunately, Dranian had no idea how to woo a female. He didn't have many elaborate words, nor was he whole in bodily strength, but he was still more powerful than the rest of the males in the building. In a fight, he could likely snap their necks with his one good arm. He wondered if Beth had noticed all that about him.

He rose from the couch and moseyed toward the door, ideas running through his mind of what he might say. He felt, "Hello, Human. Date me," and, "Shall we start invading each other's personal space?" wouldn't sound as smart as they did in his head.

Dog-Shayne slid off the couch and faithfully followed as Dranian opened the door and slid into the hall. He stared at Beth's daunting door. 3F. He stared for quite some time. He stared until he could stare no more, and he squeezed his eyes shut from the sting of not blinking for so long.

"Are you going to ask her to wed you?" Luc's voice filled the hall, and Dranian whirled.

"What? Absolutely never—not!" Dranian growled.

Luc had a swelling patch over his chin, pink and shiny. He didn't explain where he got it, he just raised a scarlet eyebrow. "Well, if you're 'absolutely never—not' going to ask her to be your bride, then why are your rhythms racing? Do you perhaps care for that clingy female?" The fox's wide, wicked grin spread across his face out of nowhere. "Please tell me you do. I would very much love to steal her from you. I'm sure I wouldn't have to try very hard."

Dranian snarled and turned to march back to his apartment, but the squeaking of an opening door filled his ears. He spun back, eyes wide, to see Beth standing in her doorway. And suddenly he forgot how to say, *"Hello."* Why though? Why did he forget? He hadn't cared a single seed what Beth thought of him until ten minutes ago.

Luc swept in, placing an arm against the doorframe with the utmost tenderness and positioning himself in such a way that he and all his obnoxious fox beauty took up most of Beth's vision. The air around him transformed into a sweet-scented lure—others would have missed it, but Dranian sniffed the wretched fox magic with his acute sense of smell. "Oh dear. Are you trying to make my heart falter, dear Beth?" Luc asked her. "Why in the world would you wear that dress and do this to me?"

It was the first Dranian noticed Beth was wearing a dress.

Beth blushed and looked down at her garment. "This thing? I was thinking of throwing it out!" she admitted.

Luc placed a hand over his chest in feign agony. "You're killing me."

Beth released a high laugh that Dranian was sure he'd never heard her use with him. He grumbled a few fairy curses and turned to leave for good, but then...

"Is that a dog?!" Beth's gasp was so loud it caught Dranian off guard. She pushed—*pushed*—passed Luc and raced to Dog-

Shayne's side, dropping to her knees to scratch behind his ears. Luc stared after her with a face that told Dranian the fox was thinking about either grabbing Beth and trying again, or simply killing her right there in the hall for refusing him.

Dranian's shoulders relaxed, and when Luc looked up from the smitten Beth, Dranian almost cast him a gloating smile. He dropped to a knee to show some affection to his beloved dog, too.

"I love dogs," Beth exclaimed, patting Dog-Shayne's head.

"As do I." Dranian admitted the revelation he'd only learned about himself in the past twenty-four hours.

"He's so cute! Can I take him for a walk sometime?" She kissed him right on the snout.

Dranian nodded.

Across the hall, Luc looked ready to explode—a strong reaction to the simple rejection. It seemed the fox wasn't having the greatest day. Dranian didn't give a fluttery fart of his time to wonder why.

"Since I ran into you two, I was actually wondering," Beth glanced over her shoulder at Luc, looking between the two fairies a few times before she spit out her request, "I have a huge dresser that needs to be moved out of my bedroom. You guys wouldn't mind, would you?" She flashed a weird smirk Dranian guessed was meant to be cute.

Dranian's almost-smiling face fell. He could already feel the burning pain that would come with trying to attempt such a physical undertaking.

Luc was smiling again. "I'm sure Dranian would *love* to assist you, dear Beth. He was just telling me how much he enjoys helping damsel humans. I imagine the dresser is... *quite* heavy."

"Aw, Dranian, you're so sweet!" Beth swatted Dranian's left arm playfully, and he bit back a croak.

Thirty seconds later, Dranian stared at the enormous dresser in horror. He swallowed the lump in his throat as he approached it under the gaze of Beth *and* Luc—the latter of whom stood by to watch. Beth's bedroom was not large, so the three of them took up most of the space, along with the mountain-sized dresser.

Dranian pursed his lips as he considered just telling Beth the truth—that all this time he had been assisting her with tasks, he had been doing it injured. He didn't know what she would think of him if he admitted it. Would she think he could no longer break her enemy's bones? Would she think of him as a less worthy male? Would she never speak to him again for keeping a secret about himself?

He cleared his throat once. Twice.

Thrice.

He squatted to try and lift the thing whole, hoping he could prop it up on his good shoulder.

"It's far too heavy to carry like that." Luc's nagging voice flitted through the room. Dranian looked back to find the fox examining a bead necklace he'd lifted from Beth's nightstand.

For someone who didn't roll their eyes often, Dranian did a rather remarkable roll of them now. He readjusted himself to wrap his arms around the dresser's middle. In one large heave, he tried to lift the thing. It came an inch off the ground.

A squeak escaped his mouth—he gritted his teeth as warm pain rippled through his bicep, into his shoulder, down to his fingers. It seemed his whole left side had lit on fire.

He dropped it.

Beth shrieked as the dresser slammed back into her bedroom floor. "The hardwood!" she complained.

Luc couldn't stifle his snort-laugh fast enough. Beth turned and swatted him so the bead necklace he held flew from his hand and bounced onto the bed. "Help him!" she demanded. "This is a two-person job!"

Luc's smile twisted into a predatory snarl. He seemed to contemplate for a split second. Then he reluctantly sauntered over and took the other side of the dresser. "Dranian might do things like this for free, dear Beth. But I require an exchange," he said before he would lift.

"An exchange? What do you need help with?" Beth shrunk back a little like the thought of scrubbing his garments clean or washing his dishes was more than she could bear—even though she seemed to have no trouble asking others to do such things for her.

"How about a romantic date?" Luc suggested. His heart-shaped lips curled into a different sort of smile. A lovely, sweet one that Dranian hated.

Beth blushed again, her moment of fear transforming into a

giggle. "I mean... okay. Sure."

Dranian thought to stomp off and leave the dresser all to Luc. But Luc suddenly lifted, and the weight of it tilted onto Dranian too fast for him to escape. He caught it, and after nearly choking on the agony of the pressure, he quickly shuffled backward out the bedroom door, Luc shimmying after him.

Beth followed, eyes glowing. She pointed to a spot by the entry. "Put it there," she dictated.

The two fairies obeyed, setting the dresser on the floor with a *thud* and less care than required. Dranian was sure his body would burst, that a tear or two might escape his watery eyes from sheer strain. But he turned back to Beth with his lips pinched tightly together, blinking away any traces of moisture before she could see it.

"You're welcome, dear Beth." Luc bowed a little. He turned to leave. "I'll be in touch about our romantic date—"

"Actually, since you're here anyway, would you mind carrying out some of these boxes to my car? I'm going to drop them all off at the thrift store tomorrow." Beth pointed to a stack of boxes in the living space. Boxes that were not all that large—ones she could have certainly carried herself.

Dranian wanted to cry a little then. He hardly cared if she saw him.

Luc though... His mouth was pressed into a thin line. His eyes narrowed upon her, and Dranian saw the moment the fox's mind changed; the very flicker of murder that entered his gaze.

"You don't mind, do you?" Beth tossed her flirtatious laugh to them as she turned around and headed to the boxes, shoving a set of earbuds into her ears. The faint sounds of music began coming from them as she scanned the box labels as if deciding which ones she wanted them to carry first.

One of Luc's fairsabers appeared. The low buzz of the blade forming burned in Dranian's ears. He hardly had time to draw his spear, sweep before the marching fox, and block his blade before it would have sliced clean through Beth.

Luc glared at her back as Dranian held him at bay. "Let me kill her, North Fairy. You want her to die now too, admit it."

Dranian nudged him back, and Luc reluctantly dropped his saber to his side, but he did not take his murderous glare off Beth's back.

Beth picked up a box and began to turn around.

Two fairy weapons retracted in a heartbeat. Two deadly handles went into pockets.

"Here," Beth said to Dranian first as she handed him a box. She pulled one of the earbuds out of her ear to tell him something important. "Be careful with this one. It's fragile."

Luc's snarl was too low to be heard by a natural human ear.

Dranian nodded once, then turned to carry the box away. But he paused by the door, waiting.

Beth handed Luc a box, too. Luc looked her up and down, not in an immodest way—more like a forest hunter who'd caught a hogbeast and was deciding how to butcher it before he ate it.

"Luc," Dranian called. His voice was dry and strained, and he hoped Beth could not hear the tone in it that told the story of how hurt he was, how every move he'd made in the last five minutes had nearly destroyed him.

Luc reluctantly tore his gaze off Beth and turned to follow Dranian out, seeming to realize that if he assassinated the building owner in her apartment, he would no longer have a place to live. He would lose, and perhaps Luc was the sort who hated to lose.

Dranian thought about that as they carried a dozen boxes to Beth's car.

He was being foolish.

Nighttime came with a whistling wind outside Dranian's bedroom window. Dog-Shayne fell asleep almost instantly at the foot of his bed. He stared up at the human realm stars, twinkling in their places. The stars seemed to ask him questions he didn't have answers to. Questions such as: *Are you daft? How could you not tell Mor that the treacherous fox of his childling years is sharing a box of space with you? How could you keep it from Cress, too, whom you swore to serve with the remainder of your faeborn life? And most of all, how could you not even call Shayne when Shayne would have certainly called you if the roles were reversed?*

Guilt prickled his insides. It was becoming unbearable.

Everything would have been easier if Shayne had just stayed

and been Dranian's roommate from the beginning.

Dranian tried to imagine his lifelong ally in his situation. But everything would have been different if Shayne was the one living with the fox. Firstly, because Shayne couldn't keep his mouth shut; he would have told Mor and Cress immediately. He would have talked Luc's ear off day and night. He might have tried to shoot the fox in his sleep already. Or he would have done what he was best at—annoy the life out of Luc with his tedious habits of singing and chatting and appearing in one's face at all hours.

If Shayne were in Dranian's situation, the matter might have already been dealt with.

Dranian wished he knew how to be annoying. He chewed on the inside of his cheek as he tapped his fingers against his phone. Even if Dranian wasn't a natural at the sport of intentional annoyance, maybe Shayne could at least talk him through the steps. Perhaps one phone call wouldn't hurt.

He quickly hit the code of buttons that would make Shayne's phone ring on the other side of their magic connection. He did it before he could change his mind. It was the first call he'd made to Shayne since the day the fellow had left to follow Greyson to the kingdom of Florida.

It rang. It rang some more.

It kept ringing.

Dranian found a voice he didn't recognize coming through the phone telling him to leave a voice message for Shayne to listen to at a later time. The thing beeped too fast, and Dranian gasped as he realized he hadn't a thing prepared to say. He blurted, "Call me!" and then he smashed his finger into the red button six times to ensure the device was no longer waiting for him to speak.

He inhaled a few times and placed a hand over his thudding heart. Then he glanced back at the stars asking all their questions.

"Hush, I'm tired," he finally told the snoopy lights in the heavens. He tossed his phone aside and laid back against his pillow. He did not fall asleep right away, but when he did, he heard a voice.

"Dranian," she said, entering his thoughts of melting colours and windy echoes. *"Don't kick me out. I need to see you. It's important."*

The being who had never even told him her name. That was the first sign she could not be trusted.

There was never a body, just whispers and the occasional reaching arm that found its way in as though she was asking him to take her hand.

Dranian's dream morphed into darker tones. Smoke, wind, and red fire. A strange sensation crawled over him; he heard shouts and screaming. He spun around over and over, but he could not seem to find where the noises came from. He curled his fists, ready to muster his energy and throw this being from his mind.

"Dranian!" She shouted this time—the loudest she'd ever spoken. *"I need to speak with you! Let me in!"* And then, *"I can chase this nightmare away if you let me."*

Not once had he replied to the voice attacking his dreams. Most souls would have answered by now, but once, a long time ago, Dranian had learned to *never* answer the call of a voice in his dreams.

He fought the impulse to shout at this being for invading in the first place. How dare she? How had she even found his mind to dreamslip into? She was probably causing the nightmare herself. It would only get worse if he said something back to her, giving her the key to enter his dreams at will.

"I've been searching every mind across the realm looking for you," she said, her volume switching from loud to almost too quiet to hear—like her connection to him was growing thin on her end.

Dranian began to push her back out as he always did. He tried, but this time, he could not seem to kick her from his thoughts. Perhaps it was because, despite his best efforts, he continued to fail to remove every being invading his faeborn life at the moment.

"Dranian, you know my voice! Don't you remember me?!" she said again quickly, and this time her words seemed to ring in Dranian's ears. He halted his efforts to send her on her way.

Remember? Had he met this mysterious voice before?

"You promised you would come back for me." This time the voice carried a blend of timidness and accusation. It was a tone that twisted something deep in Dranian's soul. A familiarity that

he had tucked away forever. *"Where are you, Dranian? What happened to you?"*

The first time he'd heard the voice, he thought he recognized it. It was certainly a trick of the dreamslipper. He was sure every time the female entered someone's dream, she made the owner feel like they knew her from somewhere. It was what dreamslippers did—persuade a being to let them in, then torment them forever with nightmares. A wicked sort of pleasure for the maddest puppet masters.

But…

But. Though it was a hazy memory from long ago, something he had forgotten about until now, Dranian did recall telling someone such a thing. Just once. In a village he had left behind. One he had never returned to.

But it couldn't be her.

This was a trap. It was also the longest he had *ever* allowed her to speak to him in his dreams.

Dranian prepared to thrust her away; his will pooled in around him as he focussed.

"Dranian!" she warned, this time with no pleading or timidness. It was a clear-cut warning. Angry. *"I have no name to tell you to make you trust me—"* He launched her from him, and she was swept backward with one limb of sound reaching back in the shape of an arm. *"You were the only one who gave me anything. Your will for me to live. A spear. Your smiles…"*

Dranian reached out and caught her arm. Her voice had almost vanished. He held her—held on as his thoughts scattered and then rushed back together again. As this faceless, bodiless being before him hung there by the thread he gripped. As his rhythms sped faster, then slower, then faster again.

As a very distinct, clear memory swept in.

"Ashi-Calla Village..." he whispered. The words came from his mouth before he realized he was saying them. He didn't mean to say them to *her*...

Suddenly a presence lunged into his dream, filling it up, blotting out all the colours as she entered, stepping out of a bright light.

Dranian gasped when he realized. He dropped her arm, he tried to reel back, but it was already too late.

She marched into his dream with a full body, coming right for him with intimidating ferocity. Dranian tried to wake himself, to escape the dream, but she grabbed his collar before he could leave.

He stared at her. At her face.

A face as terrifyingly attractive and as powerful as he could have ever imagined. He felt entirely out of control—she was in charge of his dreams now. What had he done?

"Dranian," she said in a stern voice. She didn't seem interested in sweeping him into a frightening nightmare by making him drown, or fall off a cliff into nothingness, or worse. *"I've been looking for you everywhere,"* she stated. *"I have to tell you something!"*

He blinked, even as his thoughts trembled. Even as he waited for her hallucinations of terror to consume him. He couldn't help but wonder if he'd seen her face before.

"Your friend is here!" she shouted at him, yanking his collar a little like she wanted him to shake off his daze and pay attention. *"He's going to die!"*

What had he done? What had he done? Dranian couldn't think straight.

She looked back and forth between his eyes, and her face fell. He felt a slight loosening of her grip on his collar. And he took his chance.

Dranian tore away, falling backward on purpose with nothing to catch him.

He startled awake.

Dranian sat up in bed, his chest pounding, his panting filling the bedroom. His hands became fists as every clear thought melted into a swirl, as he began to shake, as his breaths became short. As he succumbed to an illness he had not faced in a long time.

Panic. Sheer, undiluted, crippling panic.

He hardly knew what he was doing when he dragged his phone over. When he dialed Shayne's number for help. He couldn't remember where he was, but he needed Shayne.

Dranian couldn't count the number of times the phone rang. His muscles seized up as the ringing came to an end and a lady's voice invited him to leave a message. The phone fumbled out of his shaking hands and tumbled off the bed, hitting the floor with a clatter.

His bedroom door swung open.

Luc stood there, eyes half open, hair tousled like he'd awakened from a deep slumber. A lit phone was in his hand. He took Dranian in for a moment, observing his trembling. Then he held the phone up.

"Who's is this?" he asked in a raspy, sleepy voice. "It was tucked into a box of belongings hiding in my closet, and it keeps ringing."

The walls were moving. The air was suffocating him to death. Dranian could hardly register Luc's question.

He didn't see Luc enter, but suddenly Luc was there, standing by his bedside. The fox tossed the phone to the duvet and grabbed Dranian's chin, yanking his face up so Dranian locked eyes with him.

"Snap out of it, you fool," he said. "One deep breath in. One deep breath out. Repeat." His words sounded dull and uninterested, but Dranian obeyed.

One breath in.

One breath out.

In.

Out.

His spinning thoughts began to slow.

Luc dropped his chin and rolled his eyes as he left. "North Fairies," he muttered. He slammed the door behind him, and the only sounds that remained were Dranian's inhales and exhales as breathable air returned to the room.

Dranian looked down to find his nightshirt soaked with sweat where he gripped a fistful at his chest. When he realized, he released the fabric and lifted his hands to see them. They still shook, but it seemed it was no longer from panic.

He glanced toward his closed door where Luc had left. His eyes fell to the phone resting on his duvet. Slowly, he dragged it to himself, blinking back the moisture in his eyes to see it clearly. A pit sank through his stomach when he recognized the coffee mug phone case stickers and the crack down the screen.

This was Shayne's phone.

But why was Shayne's phone here?

It took Dranian a moment to recall what Luc had said when he arrived, *"It was tucked into a box of belongings hiding in my closet, and it keeps ringing."*

The only box in Luc's closet was one that held a few of Shayne's things he'd left behind when he went on his trip.

Dranian lowered the device onto his lap. He brushed a bead of sweat from his brow, and he tossed the phone onto his nightstand as it sank in that calling Shayne for help wasn't an option. That Shayne had chosen to leave his only communication device behind.

So, was Dranian really alone to face this after all?

Dranian sighed and shook out his nightshirt, letting cool air find his hot body. He was far too exhausted to feel the humiliation of Luc seeing him at the lowest point of his disability. Now the fox knew Dranian had not just one useable arm, but he also had an illness of the mind.

An illness of his lowly birth that had gotten slightly better when Shayne had showed up in his life. A disease that had only subsided when he'd come to the human realm and chose a quieter way of living among the humans.

And now… Now he'd lost control of his dreams, too.

He released a heavy breath as he realized that he could never fall back to sleep again.

11

Dranian Evelry and How it all Began
in Ashi-Calla Village, Part 2

It was hard to find the girl with no name most of the time, as she always seemed to be hiding. But Dranian crossed her here and there. She'd shoot him a subtle smile from far down the road, or she'd playfully tug a handful of his jacket as they passed each other in the street. They didn't stop to talk—that would only draw attention. But he became acutely aware when she was in view, or passing by, or busy doing something a stone's throw away.

To make things more interesting, Dranian studied at the tree-cove library and mastered the art of elftouch. She'd nearly squealed when he traced a phantom finger along the back of her shoulders from far away as he hid behind a trunk in the woods.

She'd spun with wild eyes, looking around at the woodcutter fairies chopping logs, and Dranian had nearly laughed out loud—which would have been startling enough to anyone who heard. It became a game when she noticed him hiding there. He felt a poke right back and he shrieked, alerting the woodcutter fairies all through the forest. When she did it again, it became clear she'd mastered the art of elftouch in her lifetime too, and far better than he had. He hadn't been able to scamper out of the forest fast enough as she'd poked him over and over until he was out of sight.

Dranian used his next month's coin to buy a new spear—a larger one, carved with the forest beauties of Ashi-Calla. It was strikingly magnificent and better than any other thing he owned. Weeks earlier, he would have thought he had no use for such a weapon. A half-spear would have been enough to fend off the forest creatures. But he had a strange new ambition to learn to use a full-sized weapon now. To make something of himself.

The woods became his training grounds. He fought the trunks, stabbing and slicing, and leaping high over fallen logs. He became faster at running, faster at stabbing, faster at everything with each passing day. He became obsessive, so focussed that he lost track of hours and missed work. He endured several tantrums from his father and even one from his mother who until now had hardly acknowledged his existence. He became so engrossed in the hope that he could be useful as a spear-wielder that he didn't even notice when the girl went missing.

He came back from the woods one day, drenched in sweat and

rain, his spear slick in his grip. The village roads were muddy and puddles formed in the uneven places. The rain almost drowned out the sound of the shouting males gathering around the forest hall. Dranian meant to walk by and let them be, but he glanced over, curious what all the fuss was about.

He stopped dead in his tracks when he saw one of them shove a bright-eyed, black-haired female into the log wall of the hall. She looked afraid; she looked angry.

"You little witch!" the fae spat at her. "How many of our dreams have you tried to slip into? Did you think hiding what you are would save you?"

Dranian watched in dismay as the males crouched to pick up large stones. He found himself moving toward the scene, found himself bringing his spear to life. He found himself shoving the males out of the way and standing in between them and the girl with bright eyes who had never been given a name.

The males observed Dranian's spear, one of them taking a step back. Dranian didn't know what to say—if he should announce his intentions. If he should beg for mercy. He didn't say anything at all.

"What are you going to do with that?" one of them asked with a mocking snarl. Fairy eyes narrowed on him, their new target, and suddenly clear thoughts vanished from Dranian's mind. He thought he might tip over. His heart took on a new, uneven rhythm as he felt himself trapped back in a place he had been before—the subject of their hatred.

Quiet sounds of the girl weeping came from behind him. Dranian felt his chest tighten amidst his body rejecting his control, his hands beginning to shake. One of the males easily smacked his spear away; it ripped from his grip and rolled across the ground.

"Are you really going to take these rocks, Evelry?" another male asked as he tossed his rock into the air and caught it again. "Or are you going to move out of the way?"

He should move. He should run and take the girl with him. But...

His mind fell into chaos, spinning, turning blank. He forgot where he was as his breathing became heavy and fast.

Rocks began to fly. Dranian hardly knew what he was doing, hardly remembered his own name, but one thing he did know— that this girl would die if he didn't do something. He took a rock to the shoulder as he spun around and placed his body over hers, holding his arms up to shield her face. Rock after rock pelted his back and he gritted his teeth, his mind melting and sharpening and blanking. The girl cried, whispering his name.

He did not know her name to say it back.

Only when he collapsed did the fae grow tired of it. They laughed as they walked away, and while the colours in his vision turned to blurs, Dranian lost his consciousness and was swept away into slumber.

A voice appeared on the cusp of his dream, not threatening to come in, not pushing. She just cried and said, *"Stay alive."*

Dranian could hardly move the next morning when he awoke in his bed. He wondered why his father wasn't in his room, shaking him awake, yelling at him for not being at work. He winced as he peeled back his covers and tried to stand.

When he came into the main space of the hut, he realized the rest of his family was missing, too.

"Father?" he dared to call, finding his voice dry. He swallowed and tried again, "Father?"

Still, no one answered.

Dranian came outside to blinding sunlight. His eyes stung like they were full of sand, and he lifted his arm to shield himself.

When he did, he saw his father and his mother waiting for him. Along with six fairies in rich-looking crimson robes, complete with expensive leather forest boots, jagged-edged pauldrons, and detailed threaded pictures of black land dragons across their chests. One of them held a flag with a family symbol Dranian didn't recognize.

"There he is. That's the son I was telling you about. The one who has mastered the way of the spear." His father's voice filled Dranian's ears. He felt for his pocket but realized he didn't have his spear with him. His father left the fairies in crimson to approach Dranian, and Dranian slowly lowered his arm.

"Father—?"

"You've been sold to this family as a fairy guard," his father stated matter-of-factly. Then, too quiet for the others to hear, he said, "You have shamed me in every way possible up until now. The last thing I ever ask of you is to keep your illness contained until you're long gone so they don't send you back to me."

Dranian's mouth parted. His father's claims didn't sink in—they couldn't. Because they couldn't be true. But as Dranian perceived that his father showed no signs of remorse or regret, he placed a hand over his heart where it began to thud. And thud. And... No. He could not do this. Not now; not when his father had made this one last request of him...

"Dranian!"

His head spun toward a girl racing from the forest. She had a thin green wreath in her black hair, a bruised lip, and tears in her eyes. Dranian noticed his half-spear strapped to her waist by a belt.

His father stepped in to cut the girl off, and for the first time in his faeborn life, Dranian shoved his father aside. His father blinked in surprise as Dranian strode past him to meet the girl.

He caught her. She caught him.

They caught each other.

He wanted to tell her that he'd been sold. That this was goodbye. That his father hadn't found a way to love him after all, just like she'd said. But words were hard, and so, she spoke for them both.

"I've been sold, too," she said. "Word spread through the village after those fairies found out about me. A passing merchant ship just purchased me as a slave. The captain went to see my mother as soon as he learned what I could do."

"What can you do?" Dranian asked. Still, after all this time, she'd never told him. But he shook his head. Now was not the time. "What's the name of your ship?" he asked quietly instead.

She cast him a weary smile. "You'll never find me," she promised. "The captain will use me to harm his enemies. I'll be hidden away forever, probably in a cage."

Dranian's lip curled. "The name of your ship," he said again, growling this time.

His parents called from behind him, making threats. His father would grab him soon if he didn't go.

The girl looked back and forth between his eyes, seeming to change her mind. "The Mycra Sentorious," she whispered.

Dranian filled his chest with air. "I'll work hard, and I'll become rich," he promised her. "And I will find your ship and purchase your freedom. Just hang on until then."

Dranian was torn back from her, and she was yanked the other way by the fairies in crimson. A series of hands shuffled Dranian through tall grass until he was lifted and thrown onto a reindeer. His wrists were tied and tethered to the deer's antlers so he couldn't escape.

He looked back at the girl with no name, at his childling home, at his village. He took it all in one last time as he was led away by a cavalcade of deer and beasts that would take him to his new home.

Four weeks later, Dranian got word the captain of the Mycra Sentorious had been driven mad with nightmares and had sunk his own ship to the bottom of the Twilight Lakes with his whole crew on board.

No one aboard the ship had survived.

Dranian spent eight years serving the House of Lyro, being mistreated only until Shayne Lyro, the heir apparent, decided that no fairy should be allowed to torment his fairy guard but him. The spoiled, white-haired Lord only needed to hand out a few punishments of his own—laughter-driven rampages involving the tearing out of tongues, the throwing of enchanted daggers, and the shoving of disobedient fools off the pagoda—for his new rule to stick. This one single grace gave Dranian the courage to survive; it was the security that made him have no reason to panic most days. And after a year of being a terrible guard in the beginning, Dranian Evelry from Ashi-Calla Village started to excel in his role for the first time. He became useful.

One night in his third year, he allowed himself to think of the girl with no name whom he had decided to forget about. He snuck off to the Lyro library at midnight to study "dreamslippers." It was only then he understood the magnitude of what the girl had been and why her power was so coveted and feared. It was then he understood how her ship must have gone down, too. That she had likely drowned an entire crew, along with herself. The thought left a dreadful pang in his chest. He put the book away, along with his curiosity. At least she was at peace now. At least she would never be tormented again.

When Shayne Lyro lost his title and was sent off to the Silver Castle, Dranian had nowhere else to go. So, he followed the young Lord in secret. And there, he came upon the ward of Queene Levress; a village-born fairy like Dranian, who had risen to power from nothing. The ward's name was Cressica Alabastian, and he was the greatest fighter Dranian had ever known in his young faeborn life. Watching him on the training grounds shifted something in Dranian's spirit.

From that day forward, Dranian aspired to be like the great Cressica Alabastian. He swore his allegiance, vowing to give everything he had to the Prince of the North Corner, including his life, should it be required.

Never once did he regret it.

CHAPTER

12

Luc Zelsor and the Last Thing He Wanted to See

A ballet theatre rested at the city's edge. The building was made of the finest stone that glowed silver in the morning sunlight. Inside, half a dozen twisty hallways, a large auditorium with velvet red chairs, and a wide stage with a sweeping black curtain boasted of the theatre's riches. But the best part was that the rafters above the stage were just dark enough to conceal Luc resting in them.

The fox leaned back against a pole, letting one leg dangle as he watched the dancers practice their routine below. Arched bodies morphed into spinning gods and goddesses, their pointed-toe perfection something of a marvel.

Once upon a fairy life, Luc had watched dancers such as these perform for his grandmother, the Dark Queene. His mother had shushed him when he'd tried to ask questions during the performance: *"Why are they wearing antlers? Doesn't that make it harder to dance?"* and, *"How do they glide on their toes like that?"* and, *"Can I try?"*

Luc was no dancer, to be certain. Not in comparison to the gifted fairies of the Dark Corner who had spent day and night practicing beneath the cloud of turmoil. But once or twice, while hidden away in his room, he had tried it—gliding over the floor with his fox grace—so passionately, in fact, that he drew a quiet music in from the wind and made the air taste like sugar. He'd snuck into the woods to watch the fairies dance every month after that, carefully mimicking their moves from the shadows of the emerald trees. He wanted to show his mother once he had mastered the routine.

Even after his mother had left forever, Luc had wandered back to the dancers' lair in the woods. He'd watched them to pass the time, to ease his soul, to keep himself from crying. It was his one secret refuge that his father did not know about and therefore could not destroy.

But naturally, he'd left all that behind when he'd joined the Shadow Army.

Human realm dancers were not quite as magical as fairy dancers. They could not jump as high, nor could they spin as long, nor did they have the same impressive balance. Even their costumes were bland in comparison—lacking braided wreaths, speared antlers, or awakened creeping plant dresses. But their hard work and persistence was a form of magic all on its own.

Luc rubbed his eyes as he witnessed the ballet dancers reset to begin their routine again. He wasn't much of a coffee drinker, but he wondered if he ought to indulge in one this morning to fully wake himself. He couldn't exactly complain about a bad sleep for he would never tire of sleeping on a mattress. In fact, he'd slept like an untroubled childling these last few nights since he'd moved in with the North Fairy. Curious, considering he was beyond stressed by the prospect of Mor, Cressica Alabastian, or Dranian's white-haired friend with the dirty, uncovered feet popping in at any moment for a visit.

But even with last night's drama, he appreciated his bed. The park benches had always been too hard on his back for peaceful slumber. It was the curse of being a prince—even if Luc had never recognized himself as one.

When he decided he'd had enough of the ballet, Luc swung from the rafters and landed in complete silence behind the curtain, out of sight. He glided from backstage to the emergency exit and came outside to crisp morning air tickling his nose.

Perhaps he would take a nap today. There was no reason he couldn't when he owned his own bed.

He ventured through the winding streets, searching the shops he passed for one that might promise to serve ice cream all year long. But he found no such place to ease his cravings.

Eventually he reached his building. He airslipped up to the third-floor hallway, deciding he didn't care to waste time on the code or the stairs anymore. He eyed clingy Beth's apartment door as he walked past, imagining her popping out and demanding he do more servant tasks for her. What a spoiled human she was.

He unlocked the door to 3E and went in, sensing immediately that Dranian was awake and in the kitchen. And brewing coffee. Luc sniffed a little. The delicious scent was completely muddied by the smell of repulsive, wet dog. He scowled at the mutt sleeping on a blanket in the living space as he followed his nose to the kitchen.

Dark rings surrounded Dranian's eyes when he looked up. Luc's mouth twisted as he considered addressing the incident that had happened the night before—when he'd barged in on the North Fairy having a complete meltdown. Luc had seen all sorts of panic-driven fairies back in the Army. But it was as though no one had ever taught Dranian how to overcome his spell. Perhaps none of the fools he called "brothers" even knew how to overcome such a thing.

What a herd of idiots.

Dranian turned away to watch the coffee maker as it brewed, fiddling with this and that. Tugging a mug from the cupboard. Glancing up to the top shelf for a moment to where Luc had tossed the sugar. Then he moved on and went to the spoon drawer.

"Does that always happen to you when you're overwhelmed?" Luc cut the obvious tension in the room to shreds. He was dying to know. Mostly for purely snoopy reasons.

"That's none of your business," Dranian muttered, grabbing a spoon. He took the nearby tea towel and began wiping water and coffee drips off the counter.

"It'll become my business if you continue to make a ruckus in the space I'm living in," Luc pointed out. "You severely disrupted my sleep last night. I'll take a cup of that coffee as reimbursement for my stolen slumber." He nodded toward the coffee maker.

Dranian grunted in reply, and Luc sat down at the table to wait.

"Did you have a bad dream?" he pressed.

Dranian glared back at him. "Stop that," he demanded.

"Stop what?"

"Probing."

"Oh dear." Luc sighed. "It's not probing. It's *interrogating*," he corrected. "I hate not having answers when I have questions. I plan to start cutting off your fingers soon if you don't tell me what I want to know." He smiled at himself, imagining how nice it would be if he wasn't joking.

Dranian let out a long, deep breath and leaned against the counter on his fists. "You talk too much," he muttered.

"Yes. I've been told that before." Luc nodded, flicking a gross crumb off the table.

He allowed the North Fairy several moments of silence before he spoke again.

"I'd like to make a bargain to get rid of that dog," he said.

"Dog-Shayne isn't leaving," Dranian grumbled. "He's an as-sis—"

"Yes, yes. An *assistance* dog." Luc rolled his eyes. He let out a heavy sigh. "How about I only kill one of them—clingy Beth or Dog-Shayne. You choose which one gets to live and which one must die," he decided.

Dranian ignored him as he rearranged the tea towel back over the stove handle.

Luc tapped on the tabletop. He eyed the coffee pot, almost full now.

"You haven't answered my first question," he pressed. "Do you have an episode like that every time you feel panic, or did the episodes only start when I stabbed your arm and turned you into a broken fairy—"

"I was already *a broken fairy!*" Dranian's shout shook the apartment—Luc felt the vibration beneath his feet, felt a shift in the wind, felt the distress in the growl. The mutt over in the living space whimpered.

But Luc was confused. He tilted his head as he studied the North Fairy, sure the claim didn't add up.

Dranian's chest pumped for a moment, a strange collage of emotions burning in his eyes. For someone who hardly showed reactions, it caught Luc a smidgen off guard. Dranian swallowed them down again, his expression vanishing as his jaw hardened. He abandoned the coffee pot and marched from the kitchen into his room. He slammed the door shut.

Luc nodded to himself, seeming to have found the answer he was looking for.

He rose from his seat when the coffee was finished brewing

and poured himself a large mug-full. Steam billowed up from it along with the fresh smell of ground beans. He added a pinch of milk from the fridge and reached high to yank the sugar down from its shelf. When he'd mixed his drink perfectly, he went to put everything away. The milk first, then the sugar...

He eyed the sugar. The high shelf it belonged on. Then he glanced back at Dranian's closed door.

He left the sugar on the counter beside the coffee pot instead.

As soon as Luc sat down in the living space with his delicious smelling drink, the mutt wandered over with a lapping tongue, spoiling the mood. Luc scowled at the animal. He reached for the ball sitting on the living space table. "Fetch," he said, tossing it as far away as possible in the small apartment.

The mutt leapt over the couch and raced after the ball, and finally, Luc was rid of him.

Luc sipped his coffee, looking around for the remote. He dug a hand into the crack between the couch cushions to see if it was there.

The mutt came back.

To Luc's horror, the animal dropped the drool-covered ball onto his lap. A gag threatened in the back of his throat as the wetness leaked through the knees of his pants. "You must ruin everything, mustn't you?" he asked the creature. He slumped back on the couch in surrender, flicking the ball away with the ends of his fingers.

It rolled across the floor. And again, the mutt chased after it and brought it back.

This time, Luc stared at the creature long and hard. Most animals were afraid of him this close. Most fairies were, too, and even some humans. What was wrong with this fearless animal? Slowly, Luc reached out his hand. And sure enough, the mutt dropped the ball into his palm.

It was strange, but Luc got the sense that perhaps such a creature—though too stupid to fear him—might possibly be more faithful than a fairy. Its idiocy drove it back to Luc over and over, even when Luc clearly didn't want it around. For the first time, he almost understood why humans brought them in as pets.

It was because humans could feel less stupid when there was a dog around.

Also, dogs seemed to always come back. Like an unspoken promise to never leave forever; to never abandon their owner.

Luc swallowed his disgust as he dropped the ball, then slowly reached out and patted the mutt on the head. "Dog-Shayne, is it?" he grumbled. The dog panted, gazing at Luc the same way females did when he turned on his fox charm: with complete adoration, only this wasn't forced one bit. Luc found a smile at that. "Don't flatter me so much, you mutt," he warned as he scratched the animal behind the ears the same way he'd seen Dranian do it.

He snapped when a brilliant idea filled his mind. "Shall I train you to bite?" he asked.

"Hurry *up*, North Fairy, my hands are crisping to ice." Luc held one of two tubs of ice cream toward Dranian. He shook it a little when Dranian didn't take it. Their apartment door was already wide open, and Luc wanted to avoid running into clingy Beth, lest he intentionally toss his ice cream in her face and make a scene by throwing her off the building afterward.

"I'm still getting my shoes on," Dranian mumbled, and Luc let out an impatient sigh.

Finally, Dranian had his shoes, his coat, his scowl, and his warm hat on—everything he needed—and he took the ice cream from Luc's numb fingers. He didn't look happy about going out. Though, he didn't normally look happy about anything.

"Getting some fresh air will be good for you," Luc informed him as he peeled the lid off his own tub. He began eating as soon as they were in the hall. Dranian held the door open for Dog-Shayne to follow, and they descended the stairs in a small herd.

When they came out into the fresh, late afternoon air, Luc stole a look at the grumpy North Fairy just in time to see the fool's frown lift into something a little less frowny.

Luc smiled to himself. Had he been born a human, he might have become a therapist.

Or a serial killer.

Luc's smile twisted into something else at the thought. He shook the idea from his head, deciding he should stop watching so many late-night TV shows. He always related the most to the villains in those.

There was too much ice cream eating for chatter during the first twenty minutes of the walk. When Luc was finished every last drop of vanilla sugary goodness, he tossed his empty tub into a streetside garbage barrel.

"Don't be confused by this walk, North Fairy," Luc said. "I only brought you out as a simple cure because I couldn't stand the thought of you waking me up again—should your worries drive you into another fit." He wiped his hands down his coat to remove the sticky patches. "I imagine you'll still try to kill me in three months. And I imagine I'll still kill you first."

Dranian didn't reply for a moment. Then he mumbled, "How will a walk cure me?"

Luc smiled. "Oh, trust me—"

"I don't."

"—it's already curing you. I shall sleep just fine tonight, I think." When he glanced over at Dranian, he found Dranian's brows furrowed. As though the mention of sleep disturbed the North Fairy most of all.

The wind picked up as they headed off the sidewalk and into a local park. Rain clouds began to sweep in overhead, and Luc winced up at them, hoping the sky deities would keep their spit in their mouths. Dog-Shayne barked at a prancing bug.

"Your efforts are futile. And yes, I *shall* kill you in three months to restore my honour," Dranian finally said as they headed down a path through a thick cluster of trees. They came out to another street. "My illness cannot be cured. I've searched through books and scrolls and spoken with potion brewers and fairy doctors. This is just who I am." He swallowed. Then he added, "Broken."

A slow smile spread across Luc's face. "Oh dear," he said. If only Dranian knew how ridiculous he sounded.

But it wasn't Luc's job to tell him.

A second later, a skin-tingling wind slipped over the sidewalk. Luc's feet came together.

"What in the name of the sky deities is that?" he wanted to ask aloud, but he didn't dare. His smile fled; his flesh tightened into bumps. The scent of fox blood, silver drinking water, and unquenchable greed filled the air, and for a moment, Luc forgot how to move or breathe like he was trapped in a dream. Like everything around him had shattered and he was in another place. Dranian stopped walking at his side with a strange look like he perhaps sensed something was off but couldn't peg what it was. Dog-Shayne barked like he got spooked by another bug.

But Luc knew there was no bug.

A multitude of terrified thoughts raced through Luc's mind—run, hide, fight, kill…

He could have maybe taken on the Shadow Fairies. But he could not take on *him*.

"You've had enough air, North Fairy. You and the mutt should go home now," Luc said from a dry mouth. He slid a hand into his

WANTED: A ROOMMATE WHO ISN'T EVIL

pocket where his fox bead was hidden away. He looked over at Dranian, his gaze falling upon the fool's damaged arm that would do him no good here.

Dranian didn't speak, he merely raised an eyebrow to ask why. Luc cleared his throat, feigning calmness.

"I don't think you want to be standing next to me at the moment."

The clouds turned to smoke in the sky. The wind became a torrent, brushing fallen leaves and debris into a whirl through the shop alleys and down the road. Restless humans began picking up their pace, scattering in all directions like an army was pushing them out of the way.

Which it was.

"You should leave," Luc said again, but Dranian stayed, noticing the hoard of Shadow Fairies cloaked in black plates of armour with silver-brown eyes and hatred in their souls. They were possibly too far for a fairy without fox eyes to see well, but they slid into the air and rushed in like a nest of spiders. Dranian pulled out his spear handle, and Luc shook his head.

"Don't try to fight them, you fool. They'll win," he said.

The Shadow Army drew closer, stealing the last seconds for Luc to make a decision.

Fight? Die.

Run? Live.

Forget it. He was going to fight.

Luc grabbed the spear handle from Dranian's hand. "Dog-

Shayne!" he said, making the mutt's head dart up. "Fetch!" He hurled the handle with all his might back toward the park, beyond the trees and shrubs.

Dog-Shayne lurched after it, running into the cover of the greenery. "Wait!" Dranian protested, taking three steps after his pet. He swung back to face Luc. "I can't fight without my weapon!"

"You'd better run, then." Luc shoved him toward the trees.

Dranian skittered backward a few steps, caught his balance, and glared at Luc. He couldn't seem to come up with words though. He glanced toward where Dog-Shayne had disappeared, over at the Shadow Army rushing into view with light *pops*, then back at Luc. He reached across himself, lightly touching his scarred shoulder, and he set his jaw as his glare fell away. He reluctantly jogged into the trees after his dog.

Luc waited there as the popping sounds increased, and a great, terrible army division filled the street in front and behind him. Their faces were haunted with malice, reflecting the dark shadows curling around their bones. Luc could feel their power, but it was nothing in comparison to the last fairy that appeared. The one who commanded them.

The renowned nine tailed fox himself. The mountain god of legend. Heir to the Dark throne.

His father.

Reval Zelsor appeared before Luc like a ghost, his long scarlet hair fluttering in the wind, his mouth tipped down, his dark eyes blazing with piercing silver. An oversized fairsaber was strapped to his back over iridescent black plates of armour carefully carved with fearsome words and disturbing artwork of fairies being slain.

He said exactly eight words to Luc. The son who had left him.

"Luc Zelsor. You have three days to live."

CHAPTER

13

Dranian Evelry and the Park Incident

Dog-Shayne had run off. Dranian searched the whole park, sneezing and wheezing at the overwhelming scent of Shadow Fairies. They'd smeared their odour across the air with little concern for his sensitive fairy nostrils. Those fools likely had no idea Dranian was even in the vicinity, and even if they did, he would be of no concern to them due to Shayne's bargain. But Dog-Shayne... Dog-Shayne had no such bargain with the Shadows and therefore was just as vulnerable as any creature that may have accidentally found itself in the Shadow Army's path.

Dranian checked the bushes, under the benches, behind the childling slides. He whistled. Still, the animal did not return to its master. "Queensbane," he muttered, spinning around for the hundredth time.

He released a heavy sigh and rubbed his temples. Then he glanced back toward the cluster of bushes and trees, behind which he'd left Luc to face his own problems. He wondered what had become of the fox—if the Shadow Army had taken him and were presently forcing him back through the gate into the Ever Corners. It would be a relief. Dranian would win his apartment back. Luc would be the one to have broken the contract after all these days of feuding. Dranian absolutely, without a doubt, one hundred percent, did not care.

He rubbed a hand over his chest where his heart felt a little tingly. His mind raised uninvited inquiries such as: *"Is it strange that I'm a little curious if Luc is still alive?"* and, *"What if they're trying to kill him over there?"* and *"Is the reason he dragged me out on this tiring walk today because some part of his pathological, murderous brain was a teensy tiny bit concerned for my well being?"*

It didn't matter. Dranian didn't care.

Yet… His wretched eyes couldn't stop staring at those bushes. He tilted a pointed ear toward them just a fraction, trying to pick up any sounds or stories in the air of a nine tailed fox struggling or fighting or bleeding.

Dranian jumped in surprise when a red-haired being burst from the shrubs followed closely by a panting dog with its tongue hanging out. Luc was swaying his arms in all directions like a maniac.

"Run!" the fox yelled, and Dranian was sure he'd never seen the fool's silver-brown eyes so wide and desperate. "Run, you idiotic, ever-scowling, useless North Fairy!" He and Dog-Shayne raced right by Dranian standing there. Dranian blinked, and then he chased after them.

Two fairies and one dog sprinted over the grass, through an alley, and leapt into a busy street at full speed. Dranian knocked a childling's ice cream off its cone as he twisted to try and keep himself from pummelling humans. Luc almost tripped over a stroller being pushed by a young female. Dog-Shayne stopped running and started licking the glob of ice cream on the sidewalk as the childling began to wail. Luc whistled, and the dog started running again.

They wove around couples and crowds of youth in uniforms. Dranian realized Dog-Shayne had patches of red on his fur that looked suspiciously like blood.

"Take my hand!" Luc shouted at Dranian.

"Absolutely not! Are you mad?!" Dranian returned in disgust.

Luc gritted his teeth and tried to snatch Dranian's hand as they ran. Dranian did everything he could to avoid it. There was smacking and pulling of sleeves and shoving. But in the end, Luc got a grip on Dranian's pinky finger. He held on tight and reached for Dog-Shayne.

The triad was sucked into the wind, and Dranian's faeborn heart doubled over. He kept his eyes wide open as they sped through streets and buildings and even a few unsuspecting humans.

They landed on wobbly feet a few blocks from where they'd been.

Dog-Shayne barfed up his ice cream.

Dranian whirled on Luc. "What happened?!" he asked, spotting a bead of sweat upon Luc's temple.

Luc leaned forward with his palms on his knees, catching his breath. He looked up to meet Dranian's gaze this time, revealing bloodshot eyes, dirt, and more sweat. "Oh dear. It's a long, uninteresting story," he admitted.

"Well, you're going to tell it to me," Dranian demanded. "And why is my dog covered in blood?!"

Luc made a face and stood. "It's not *his* blood—"

"I don't care *whose blood it is!*" he snapped. "That is *my* assistance dog! And you don't like him! How dare you use him to fight your battles!"

Luc released a diabolical laugh. "I didn't force him to do it. The mutt raced over at the first sign of trouble." He took the leash and patted Dog-Shayne on the head. "We make a good team, actually."

Dranian snatched Dog-Shayne's leash and tugged the dog back. "You absolutely do not! Dog-Shayne and *me* make a great team!"

"Dranian?"

Both fairies stiffened at the sound of a new voice. They turned in unison to find a blue-eyed human female standing on the curb beside a parked police vessel with a swirling iced coffee in her fingers. Her sleeves were rolled up, revealing layers of artwork on her flesh.

"Queensbane," Dranian muttered as he took in Lily staring at him in question. Her hair had grown so much this past year, she wore it in a long, blonde ponytail that reached almost to her hips, making her look even more comely and a smidgen more menacing with her she-strength and no-nonsense ways. If one squinted their eyes, they might even mistake her for a fae.

Dranian was all too aware of the fox at his side. The one he had failed to tell Mor about. The one he had failed to mention to a single one of his allies at Fae Café, including Lily Baker.

Lily dropped her coffee to the sidewalk and drew her gun. Dranian hardly knew what he was doing as he swept into the crossfire, coming so close to her weapon that it nearly pressed against his heart. Lily's mouth parted as she looked up at him in disbelief.

She quickly dropped her gun back to her side. "Are you crazy, Dranian?" she accused.

He wasn't sure if she was mad he'd moved into the crosshairs of her weapon or because she'd caught him red-handed with Luc. Realistically, either crime was worthy of a buttocks beating.

Dranian raised his hands in hopes of calming her, but the gesture only seemed to offend her more. "It's not what it looks like, Human," he swore.

An arm came around his shoulders. "Actually, it's exactly what it looks like, *Human*," Luc's sweet voice declared. "This North Fairy and I are roommates now. We even have a dog together."

Dranian blanched. He shook Luc's arm off.

The sound of disbelief that came from Lily was one Dranian had never heard before. She put her hands on her hips. "Really, Dranian? Him?" She blinked with all the indignation and raging fire of the sky deities. "Seriously?"

"He's lying—"

"Would you like to see our apartment as evidence? It's not far from here," Luc invited.

Dranian glared at him. "Take Dog-Shayne home. Later... we'll have words." He articulated the promise and shoved Dog-Shayne's leash into Luc's hands.

Lily blinked at the leash in disbelief.

"Oh dear." Luc tapped a finger along his chin. "I would, but I think I'd rather get the High Court of the Coffee Bean involved in all this now," he said, and Dranian's face changed. Luc looked down and nudged a pebble on the sidewalk with his toe. "Wouldn't hurt," he added with a murmur.

"What?!" Dranian and Lily both asked at once.

"It's that or the division will kill me." Luc held up Dog-Shayne's leash. "*And* the dog," he added. "We've both offended them greatly."

Dranian stared with his mouth hanging open.

It was Lily who finally moved first. She reached for Dog-Shayne's leash. "I'll take him, and I'll keep him safe at the—"

Luc yanked the leash back and held it up high where she couldn't reach. He was quite tall, and when Lily looked up the length of his arm, a broad smile spread across his face. "Oh dear. Too short," he said.

Lily spoke through her teeth. "I really don't like you," she told him.

"I don't like you, either," Luc promised. Then he *winked*, and Lily looked like she might claw out his faeborn eyes.

But Dranian stared off at nothing, his feet stuck in place. "We can't bring in the High Court of the Coffee Bean," he stated quietly, making both Lily and the fox turn their heads toward him.

"Why not?" Lily and Luc spoke in unison this time. Luc smiled at Lily again, revelling in it.

"I've deceived Mor. He will feel betrayed," Dranian mumbled.

"Serves him right," Luc said.

Lily gave up on the leash and turned to Dranian with folded arms. "If you're really living with this guy, you have to tell the others *now*. Dranian, he tried to kill Mor! He attacked Violet! This guy isn't our friend!" She pointed at Luc with her thumb.

"You don't have to say it right in front of me," Luc muttered. "And both of them were fine in the end." He said the last part more to himself as he looked himself over and began wiping off purple fairy blood.

"I cannot tell them until I've taken my apartment back by myself," Dranian stated. "I must do this. Or I'll never be able to face anyone again!"

Lily released a heavy huff. "Why, Dranian?"

"Because if I fail now, I'll always be considered *useless!*" He shouted it—on accident, but fire moved through his veins. He wasn't one to raise his voice; it felt strange on his own tongue. And it startled Lily.

She looked at him with wide, human eyes, suddenly seeming very delicate.

"I apologize," Dranian choked out. "I'm just trying to restore my honour." He expected Luc to laugh or snort or mock, but no sound came from the nine tailed fox.

Lily put her hands on her hips. She paced around in a small circle. She ran a hand through her hair, dislodging a few strands and ruining its neatness. She turned back to face him.

"Do you realize what you're asking of me?" she said. "You're asking me to keep a secret from everyone. Including Kate." Her gaze flicked over to Luc. "And I don't trust him. You're injured, Dranian. He can hurt you any time he wants."

Her words felt cold as they moved through Dranian's mind and body.

"You're injured, Dranian. He can hurt you any time he wants." It raced through thrice over before he managed to move a muscle, and he swallowed.

Injured.

"You're injured."

She might as well have agreed that he was useless.

But she was right. Luc could have hurt him any time he'd

wanted. And that sank in, bringing other questions. Truly, it was in a fox's nature to kill a problem, and Luc was powerful enough to have murdered everyone in the apartment building by now. He could have ruled over all the spaces, living alone in lovely, quiet bliss.

Yet, last night Luc had crossed the threshold into Dranian's room. The nine tailed fox had *been there* during Dranian's panic spell. Then this morning, Luc had insisted Dranian come outside for some air.

"I don't think he plans to harm me," Dranian told Lily, surprising himself with the news.

Lily closed her eyes in disbelief. She scuffed her hair with her fingers again.

"Please keep my secret," Dranian added, taking Lily by the shoulders so she would stop anxiously pacing. "I shall deal with this," he swore. "Mor doesn't need to know."

Lily stared for several seconds. "Come with me," she finally said. She turned and headed toward her police vessel. She opened the passenger side door and waited. "I'm not taking you to Fae Café," she promised.

Dranian slid his jaw back and forth as he contemplated. He glanced over at Luc, and Luc shrugged like he didn't want to get involved—which was a drastically different implication than a second ago.

"I'm only going to keep your secret if you come with me. I'm taking you somewhere that'll give me some peace of mind if you're going to be like this," Lily clarified. She cut Luc a look. "You stay."

Luc snorted a laugh and wrapped Dog-Shayne's leash twice around his fingers. "See you at home then, North Fairy," he said to Dranian. Then a little more seriously, he added, "Don't stay out too long. Dog-Shayne and I only have a few days left to live." He reached for the dog, and a second later they both vanished, leaving Dranian there gaping like a fool.

He spun to Lily. "Did you hear that?!" he asked, pointing at where Luc just was. "Insolent fool," he growled. "He'd better take care of my dog!" He marched across the sidewalk and slid into the passenger seat of Lily's vessel.

The drive wasn't long, but Dranian almost dozed off. He jerked his head up when he realized, slapping a hand over his faeborn heart, and making Lily jump in the driver's seat. His chest pounded—he'd almost slipped away into the nightmare world. The world he had created for himself when he'd done the unthinkable and responded to a dreamslipper's call.

"What's wrong with you?" Lily asked, arching a brow. "You're freaking me out."

Dranian closed his eyes and didn't reply until his heart settled. Then he said, "I'm being haunted by a ghost."

Lily made a weird face. "Seriously?"

Dranian rubbed his eyes, his forehead, his temples. "Yes. A being entered my dreams last night, impersonating someone who's dead. It's an obvious trap, and now I can never fall asleep again as long as I live."

Lily was quiet for a few seconds. Then she asked, "Is that a fairy thing? Can you actually live without sleep?"

Dranian almost spoke several times. He finally settled on a simple, "No."

Lily pulled the vessel to a stop, and Dranian leaned to see out the window, taking in the height of the monstrous building. It was so tall, it seemed to brush the clouds. A large sign wrapped the front that read: DESMOUNT TECH INDUSTRIES.

"I've never heard of this mysterious place," Dranian mumbled. He climbed from the vessel and followed Lily to a wheel with tall panels of glass at the front of the building. He watched in amazement as she pushed against one of the panels, and all the attached panes revolved. Lily glanced back, seeming to realize Dranian hadn't followed as the glass sucked her into the building. A panel of glass followed her, sealing her away in a cozy coffin of space.

"Get in!" she called, her voice muted through the glass.

Dranian gazed at the moving panels as they went by. He took a small step toward a moving gap but hesitated, and the glass swooshed past, sealing him out again. He huffed and reached to stop the doors from moving so he might stand a chance. He caught a panel of glass just as Lily hopped out on the other side, safe and sound. The whole contraption screeched to a loud halt.

Humans in the building seemed to pause their chatter to see what the commotion was as Dranian stepped inside carefully. He looked at Lily through the barriers. "How do I make this enchanted glass obey?" he murmured to her, not loudly enough. Lily raised both hands, seeming to wonder what he was doing and why he was still standing there.

So, Dranian eyed the glass panel before him. He pushed against it as Lily had done. The whole thing began to rotate, and he leapt ahead in alarm, pressing himself flat against it so the panel chasing him didn't catch up. His faeborn nose was squished, his mouth pressed flat. He tried to communicate with Lily through the clear pane, but all it did was smoosh his lips around.

When he saw an opportunity, Dranian broke from the glass cage in a great leap, landing before Lily in relief. He rose to stand, casting a little glare back at the revolving glass panels that had nearly taken him hostage. "I shall never try that again," he swore. When he glanced back at Lily, he didn't find her looking proud that he'd beaten the obstacle course. Rather, she was pinching the bridge of her nose.

"Unreal," she breathed. "Even after a year of living here, you guys still find ways to embarrass me."

Without another word, she turned and headed toward a brightly lit lobby, ignoring the stares and questioning looks of the humans scattered around the space. She pulled a card out of her pocket and tapped it against a pad. A small, waist-height magic gate opened, allowing them to enter.

JENNIFER KROPF

Dranian followed Lily to a set of metal doors. A shiny button was beside it, and Lily reached to press it but hesitated. She glanced back at Dranian in thought. Then she said, "We should probably take the stairs." She headed to a tall white staircase, muttering, "If you can't handle revolving doors, I don't want to see what'll happen to you in an elevator."

Everything got a little darker upstairs. They entered a long hallway and Lily pushed through a door into a room with no windows. Dranian blinked to adjust his fairy vision as his gaze fell upon various things hung up, evenly spaced apart along the walls. He studied them curiously, trying to imagine what they might be. Diagrams also filled bright screens depicting... depicting...

"What in the faeborn-cursed human realm is this?" Dranian felt his blood warm. His eyes narrowed on those diagrams of figures with pointed ears. His eyes darted to a table in the middle of the room covered in loose parchment. He read a few titles, gathering quickly what they were about.

This was a research lair. These diagrams were of fairies. Those things hanging on the walls... Weapons. Terrible weapons. Weapons meant to kill fairies.

"Queensbane, Lily Baker, where have you brought me to?" Dranian felt the blood drain from his cheeks as he growled. He stopped walking, considering leaving the way he'd come. Considering destroying everything in this room first.

Lily turned to face him, her hand finding his shoulder. Her grip was strong.

"This is for your safety," she stated. She reached over and pulled a small weapon off the wall. A gun—like hers.

"You need to take a sample of Luc Zelsor's blood and put it in here." She let go of Dranian's shoulder and pointed to a small chamber on the weapon. "Just a pin prick will do. Then you'll be able to shoot him, even if he airslips. In fact, with one Shadow Fairy sample, you'll be able to shoot *any* Shadow Fairy. The stun bullet will follow them, even at superspeed."

Dranian gaped at her. He could not fathom it, nor could he come up with the words appropriate to scorn her for this thing she was doing.

"I've been working on this since what happened last Christmas," Lily clarified at the look on his face. As if her specifying would change her betrayal. "I had to do something, Dranian," she added, quieter this time. She turned and began disassembling the weapon on the table, checking its parts, "after what happened to Kate." She swallowed, her slender throat bobbing slightly as she began putting the weapon back together. "It's my job to protect her. This is the only way I know how."

Dranian's body was still tense and icy, but his shoulders deflated an inch. So this was why Lily had been hoarding all those myth and legend books all these months. It was why she'd been absent from Fae Café so many evenings. "Does Mor know you've created a deadly bullet that can chase him through the wind?" he asked through his teeth. "Does my brother have any idea you've created a weapon that can destroy him?"

Lily looked down, hiding the guilt on her face. But she didn't look like she regretted what she'd done. "I would never use this on him."

"It doesn't matter, Human. Someone else might," Dranian growled.

"The bullets don't kill, they *stun*. And I would never let someone use this on Mor, or any of you." Lily sighed and handed him the gun. "Use this to defend yourself. I'll feel better about keeping your secret if I know you have this."

Dranian didn't take it.

"I'll tell Mor what you've been up to if you don't keep this with you," Lily threatened instead.

Dranian's jaw tightened. He reluctantly reached out and took the vile, horrid thing Lily had created. "I won't use it," he vowed. "I shall destroy it."

Lily rolled her eyes and turned back to the table to straighten up the papers there. She grabbed a pen and scribbled on one. Dranian took the opportunity to steal a look at all the abominations on the walls. "What does that one do?" he asked, pointing to a particular mechanism that looked like a satchel. He bit his mouth shut as soon as he said it, wishing he'd never spoken. He was not interested in weapons that targeted fairies.

Lily glanced up though. "That's a flame gun," she said, looking right back down at her notes. "It shoots fire."

Dranian blinked. "Like a dragon?"

A smile cracked over Lily's face. "Yes. Like a dragon."

Dranian studied the thing. It had two straps that seemed to hug one's shoulders, a satchel that rested upon one's back, and a large tube that ran from the satchel to a wide-mouthed gun. "How absurd," he muttered in an uninterested tone. "How far does it shoot the fire?"

Lily finished her writing and stood tall. "It could probably shoot halfway across this building," she said.

Dranian's jaw dropped. He slammed it closed immediately.

"That's not interesting at all," he stated. He took one last look at the fire breather. Then he turned and headed for the door with his new fairy-targeting gun. "And I won't be using this." He held the gun up between his thumb and forefinger like it contained an infectious disease.

"Do I need to call Shayne and get him to talk some sense into you?" Lily threatened again. "I might have agreed to keep your secret from Mor, but I won't keep it from Shayne."

"Ha!" Dranian turned back and waved a finger at all the weapons on the walls. "You'd have to admit *your* treachery if you were to call Shayne about this."

Lily opened her mouth to reply like she had something to say about that. But she closed it again and bit her lips. A second later, she turned back to her papers. "Shayne's been giving me the cold shoulder since he left," she admitted. "But I'll get him to talk to me in order to rat you out."

Dranian snarled and *nearly* smiled. "Alright, Human. Go ahead. Try calling him." He thought of Shayne's phone tucked safely away in his apartment.

Lily made a disbelieving sound as she pulled out her phone to call his bluff. She hit the necessary buttons and held the device to her ear. Dranian heard the faint sound of ringing, and he huffed a dry almost-laugh.

"Hello?" someone answered, and Dranian's almost-smile fell.

"Hey Greyson. Can I talk to Shayne?" Lily asked.

Dranian took a fast step forward. "Wait," he said, reaching for her phone as Greyson's muted response came. Lily's face changed as she stepped back, avoiding Dranian's grabby hands.

"What do you mean, he's not there?" Lily said into the phone. "You mean he's not in the room with you, or…" Something changed on Lily's face, bringing Dranian's attempt to wrestle the phone from her human fingers to a stop.

"If he's not in Florida, then where is he?" she asked. The faint sound of Lily's elevated rhythms found Dranian's ears, and Dranian dropped his hand back to his side.

Lily mumbled a goodbye of sorts and hung up her phone. She had a strange look on her face when her velvety blue gaze slid back up to Dranian's.

"Shayne's not in Florida," she said like she didn't believe her own words. "Greyson said he cancelled at the last minute and didn't go. He hasn't been there the whole time."

Dranian stared.

Shayne…

Wasn't in Florida.

Didn't take his phone.

Hadn't told a soul where he was… for *weeks*?

The fairy-targeting weapon grew heavy in Dranian's hand. His faeborn chest tightened like he was forgetting how to breathe… and that never ended well. He forced a large breath deep into his lungs, and he blew it out slowly.

The fool. The always smiling, shoe hating fool. Dranian's voice was a low growl when he spoke again. "Where in the name of the sky deities is he?"

Dranian banged open the apartment door of 3E and marched in.

Luc stood there, seemingly waiting. The fox didn't speak. Whatever humour had been on Luc's face before was gone now. Swelling bruises and fresh cuts marked his neck and face—things Dranian hadn't noticed back in the street while they'd been running from the park.

Dranian wanted to ask, *"What do you mean you and Dog-Shayne only have a few days left to live?"* but Luc seemed to read his mind.

The fox marched to meet him in the middle of the room. He put a hand on Dranian's temple, and Dranian's surroundings changed—his mind filling with a mostly black and white memory, only certain colours coming through; red, pink, and a few notes of blue. Dranian became aware he was seeing a memory through Luc's eyes.

A menacing, scarlet-haired fairy cloaked in dark armour stood before him.

CHAPTER

14

Luc Zelsor and the Thing that Happened at the Park
Four Hours Ago

The presence of Shadows coated everything in a thin layer of frost and fear. Luc fought a shudder from that all-too-familiar feeling. He'd been living in the luxury of freedom for too long. He'd briefly, blissfully forgotten what it was like to live in the darkness.

His father was a vision of destruction before him, cloaked in horrors from his lifetime of torture, chaos, and annihilation. A cruel fairy. A fairy who wanted nothing more than to rule over a cruel son.

Three days. Luc wondered how far he could run in three days. How much chaos and how many terrors he could cause in just three days. He wondered if he could slay this entire division in that time, before they came to collect the lives they planned to steal.

But, alas, his father was the one adversary he would not, *could not* face.

"Three days?" Luc mused anyway. "How unfortunate."

Prince Reval's robes fluttered in the cold wind beneath his armour. He said nothing more. His face was a detached, hollow shell. No longer a father. No longer an ally.

Ten Shadow Fairies marched around the High Prince, carrying with them a thin wristlet of branches with three white blossoms woven in. Luc swallowed as he considered what each of those blossoms meant. He raised a finger, halting the fairies before they could bind him to that fate.

"Let's make a bargain, Father," he tried. "If I bring you a report of all my findings in the human realm and fulfill my tasks like a dedicated scout should, perhaps we can just put this all behind us? I am your flesh and blood, after all. I am heir to the Dark throne. Has the Queene no compassion left for her beloved grandson?"

It pained Luc to remind his father of that. He hated the words "flesh and blood" and "heir" and "Dark throne." They were poison on his tongue. He would rather watch the aging Dark Queene be tossed into a damp pit of water beasts than admit she was his grandmother, but here he was. Doing it.

One of the Shadow Fairies at Luc's left cleared his throat, pulled out a scroll, and began to read. Reval did not take his piercing eyes off Luc.

"Luc Zelsor, you have been ex-communicated from the

Shadow Army," the fairy began, and Luc's lips thinned. He shifted his footing, marking the best possible directions to run. "You have been black-marked as a traitor for fleeing your post, and you shall therefore be stripped of your position. Your remaining fox lives will be taken in three days' time. No longer shall you be referred to as a Shadow Prince—"

"We all know I was never a Shadow Prince," Luc muttered.

"—and no longer shall you have the Queene's favour. You shall die a shameful death by strokes of cold iron, and any fairies who attempt to aid you from here on in shall die at your side, equally as shamefully."

Luc smirked at that one. As if any fairy would care enough to do that.

When the Shadow Fairy was finished reading, he rolled the scroll and slid it away. Reval had not blinked since the moment he'd arrived. As soon as the announcement was finished, he turned his back on Luc.

It felt as though a stone sank through Luc's chest, crushing his heart flat. Its weight grew heavier as Reval disappeared into the swarm of Shadow Fairies. As he vanished into the air, leaving Luc to the division.

It took all Luc's might to force a broad smile across his face. He addressed the Shadows inching in, holding out the wristlet. "Fools," he said. "The Prince didn't even stay to help you get that on me." He nodded to the wristlet. "You're all going to die trying."

A loud ruckus erupted from the streetside. To Luc's surprise,

Dog-Shayne came racing in, snarling and growling at the Army. Luc hid his laugh. "Good boy," he said as Dog-Shayne joined him at his side. The Shadows studied Dog-Shayne like they didn't know how to approach him.

"Dog-Shayne," Luc said, patting the mutt on the head. He lifted his hands and snapped his fingers. "*Bite.*"

Dog-Shayne growled and lunged, digging his fangs into the nearest fairy's leg—the one who held the wristlet. The fairy screamed and panicked, swatting at the mutt. Without thinking, he shoved the wristlet toward the dog, and the wood's magic wrapped around the dog's neck like a collar instead. Luc laughed as the Shadow Fairy seemed to realize what he had done.

Luc struck first. His knuckles broke through a fairy's jaw. He airslipped backward—just three feet and out of reach—any longer in the wind would have made the entire army take chase. He reached into his pocket, his smile widening as he pulled out a glistening ruby and slid it into his mouth. Perhaps a small part of him had missed this deliciously violent chaos.

Luc drew his fairsaber as a fairy charged. He thrust, his blade forming inside the fairy. He tore it back out and went for the next as Dog-Shayne bit into fae flesh left and right. A Shadow tried to stab the hound, but Luc was there, his fairsaber blocking the blade.

Luc and Dog-Shayne whipped through the Army like a gale, too distracted to notice a Shadow pull out a second wristlet. In seconds, dead division fairies covered the sidewalk, their bodies rolling onto the road. Luc stepped over them and Dog-Shayne trotted up the piles, barking at the top like the great conqueror he was. Luc laughed horridly.

Just until he was grabbed from behind by three sets of hands and dragged to the ground, his fairsaber kicked aside.

That was where Luc stopped giving Dranian the memory.

The recollection fizzled away, bringing Luc and the North Fairy back into the apartment. The sound of coffee chugging through the machine in the kitchen filled Luc's ears, the smell of the neighbour's cooking tickled his nostrils. His mouth was dry; his throat felt thick.

Dranian didn't say a word, but his jaw remained hard. It seemed he didn't quite know what to ask as he opened his mouth and closed it again. The grumpiness and resentment had left his face the moment Reval Zelsor had appeared in the memory.

"You've been mistaken about something this whole time, North Fairy," Luc said, his voice raspy and quiet. "You believe yourself to be broken because of your arm. Because of your *fits*." He twisted his mouth and dropped his gaze to the floor. "But I've analyzed thousands of fairies. I've made a study of brokenness, of inadequacies. And you see, a truly broken fairy... that looks a lot more like me."

Dranian drew back. Luc had learned the fairy wasn't one for speeches to begin with, but it bothered him more than usual now. Dranian looked like a startled reindeer.

Luc could have been humiliated by the wretched face-to-face experience with his father. There was no way the North Fairy hadn't recognized who Reval Zelsor was to Luc with his scarlet fox hair and deadly eyes that mimicked his own.

Dranian seemed to realize he was staring. He finally dropped his attention to Luc's arm as if wondering if the Shadow Fairies had succeeded in trapping him. His gaze fell upon the bracelet of branches with three fresh blossoms hugging tight to Luc's wrist. The truth appeared heavy as he took that in. He looked like he might make a comment about it. But instead, he asked, "Are you colour blind?"

A slow smile found Luc's face. "Mostly."

Dranian folded his arms. His natural scowl returned. "Why did Dog-Shayne attack those fairies? He's loyal to me, not you."

Luc looked toward the kitchen where the sounds of Dog-Shayne's panting could be heard. "He's loyal to me, too," he said. Then he pulled a shoulder into a shrug. "And I fed him an enchanted thistle."

Dranian's arms tightened around himself. "You fed him a thistle?!"

"Yes. He gagged a little trying to eat it, but he got it down. Truthfully, I just wanted to see if I could make him bite you whenever I snapped my fingers. I wasn't planning to make him fight, but now that he has—"

"You've doomed my dog," Dranian stated. "He's been bound to the stability of three delicate blossoms, and now the Shadows

WANTED: A ROOMMATE WHO ISN'T EVIL

will track him with that wristlet and kill him in three days alongside you!"

Luc scratched the back of his head and looked at something on
the wall that seemed particularly interesting.

"How shall I stop that Dark Prince from killing Dog-Shayne?"
Dranian asked.

Luc cast him a weak smile. "My father cannot be stopped, unfortunately. If there was a way to do it, I would have figured it out
by now," he said.

"That doesn't make sense," Dranian objected. "No fairy is in-
vulnerable. That's the Brotherhood of Assassin training for *begin-
ners*. Queensbane, what is your father holding over you that for-
bids you from killing him and being free?" He unfolded his arms.

Luc stared at the North Fairy for a moment. Roommates or not,
Dranian Evelry was still the enemy. Most hours, Luc still thought
about killing him. Even though Luc had allowed the fool to see
the complicated mess of his relationship with his father, Dranian
could not be trusted with Luc's deepest secret—and that was
something Luc knew better than to forget. "I told you. It's a long
story," he deflected.

Dranian growled a huff. "Well, I have my own fairy problems
now. I have a scheming brother to hunt down, and I can't leave
until I know Dog-Shayne is safe. So, you're going to tell me the
long story so we can deal with this, and I can leave in peace."

Luc's lip curled into a snarl. "No," he said, "I'm not."

"Don't be unreasonable, Luc," Dranian threatened. "I'll save my dog, even if I have to interrogate the answers out of you. This is not a negotiation!"

Luc laughed, the swelling on his lips pulling with the motion. "Oh dear. You're on your own then, North Fairy," he said. "Though I would have loved to see a three-legged guard dog try to interrogate a fox."

To prove his decision, Luc vanished.

Cold wind rushed against him when he appeared on the rooftop of the apartment castle. He folded his arms, his forefinger tapping against his bicep.

He stood there all night, thinking. Staring at the blossom-adorned wristlet. His death sentence. Looking out into the vast sky that stretched further than even his sharp fairy eyes could see. He wondered what was beyond those buildings and hills and gusts of wind. He wondered if he would live to see it all.

He wondered just how fast his fairy magic could take him to a distant land where no one would know his face.

CHAPTER

15

Luc Zelsor and the Long Story

The truth was, it wasn't a long story. Luc Zelsor was simply a pathological liar.

All it had taken was one very short conversation, and Reval Zelsor had Luc in his grips for the rest of his faeborn life.

"I found your mother after all these years." Those were the words Reval uttered as he approached Luc from behind on an evening three short years ago. The silver moon shone brightly, and the forest crickets sang a sharp, ear-piercing tune. Luc had been sorting shellfish, but his hands froze upon the sapphire clams. He didn't dare turn and look at his father, but his ears tilted, wide open, listening. "I've put her somewhere."

"Where?" Luc's mouth betrayed him. He should not have

asked or made it seem like he cared.

Reval was quiet for several moments. "It's a secret, Luc. But not to worry; I lower food through a hole so she can eat. It's quite dark, but your mother has always survived in darkness."

Luc swallowed the hard lump in his throat. There were more questions he wanted to ask, but he fought his impulses and stayed quiet. He was admitting too much with each peep he made.

The Dark Prince's cold monstrosity felt more enormous than normal as he took a step closer to Luc's exposed back. Luc watched as his father's shadow engulfed his in the grass before him.

"It's a safeguard," Reval stated in his sweet, icy voice, "so you can never turn against me, Son."

Luc nearly dropped the sapphire clams. He grabbed a pot like he'd been intending to anyway, and he tossed each clam in one by one, keeping busy.

"Now, if I ever die, she will starve to death. You understand, right?"

Luc turned to face his father. They were the same height now, almost the same build. Reval's power was treacherously horrifying but Luc had grown strong. Possibly strong enough to give him a good fight, maybe. Clearly strong enough to worry him.

Every ounce of Luc's fairy flesh worked to put a broad, crystal-clear smile upon his face that could not be read as anything but assurance. "I would never betray you, Father."

It was a lie. Luc would have. Right up until that moment, Luc had dreamt of the day he might grow strong enough or clever enough to outsmart and destroy the man who had ruined him.

But it seemed Reval had been more clever than Luc that night; had been one step ahead of him all along. That evening the young nine tailed fox decided he would run away instead. A plot of destruction transformed into a plan of escape in the blink of an eye.

It took Luc over two years to get the permission he needed to leave the Shadow Army's daily routine to become a scout among the humans. Two years of hard work, lying, bribing, cunning strategy, being in the right place at the right time, placing bets, making bargains, and giving away large promises.

Two years before he made it to the human realm.

And there, he had hoped to be free of fox games forever.

THE
BACKSTORIES
THE &
FRONTSTORIES

CHAPTER

16

The Girl with No Name

Lightning and thunder filled the cloudy skies on the dark evening the Mycra Sentorious sank to the bottom of the cold Twilight Lakes. The waters rumbled back at the heavens in response with the spraying and crashing waves. The wind screamed too, adding to the angry chorus. The chaos was so great that not even the sky deities would have noticed a young girl with onyx-black hair treading water in the middle of the lake. The force of the sinking ship tried to suck her down with it, but she was far enough away that she could withstand the pull. She had begun her swim at dusk, after all.

The raging waters had shoved her under more than once bringing back memories of a time when she'd nearly drowned in a river, and a sweet, soft-spoken boy had leapt in to save her. That day, she'd decided she would learn to swim.

She stroked against the pressure now—it was her versus the lake.

Her spirit nearly gave up, and she wondered why she had even tried until a tiny light appeared in the distance. The girl shed a tear in relief as a small boat struggled to stay right-side-up against the waves. She waved to it.

"I'm here!" she called.

The boat picked up speed, rattling the metal lantern hanging out front. It reached her with seconds to spare—the girl was sure she would have drowned if the boat had taken any longer to reach her.

A silver-haired Shadow Fairy gazed down at her curiously from the boat. After a moment, he said, "I had convinced myself none of this was real. But you are real, aren't you?"

"Help me!" the girl called to him, reaching for the fairy with her last ounce of strength.

The Shadow Fairy smiled and shook his head in disbelief. He reached for the girl and tugged her from the lake in one great haul. The girl landed in the boat, coughing up water and weeds. When she caught her breath, she whispered, "Thank you for coming."

The Shadow Fairy nodded as he turned his boat around and began paddling back the way he had come. "I don't do favours for free," he said. "You tricked me into giving you control of my slumbers, Siren."

The girl climbed to her knees and held the side of the boat as the ride grew turbulent. "I'm not a siren," she said.

"You have the power to deceive, and I found you floating in the dark waters. You convinced me to pull you into my boat. Sounds like a siren to me." He was making a jest, but the girl didn't have the will to laugh.

"I told you in your dream that I'd be here. I hardly think you can claim to have stumbled upon a siren in the water." She wrung out her hair, but it did little as the air grew heavy with mist. Rain began to soak them all over again.

"I wonder what your story is, that you had to trust a Shadow Fairy to help you escape? My species aren't known for keeping our promises. I could steal your memories, you know," the Shadow said.

The girl thought about that for a moment as her breathing finally began to settle. "I need to find someone." That was the only answer she gave him.

"That's unfortunate," the Shadow Fairy said as he stroked along with the waves. The current was moving with them now, rushing the boat toward the faraway shore. So, the fairy dropped the paddle into the boat and let the water do the work. He turned to the girl.

"Why is that unfortunate?" the girl asked.

The Shadow Fairy laughed. A crack of thunder blotted out the end of his chuckles, but he bit his lower lip over a grin. "Because you'll forget all about that person in no time."

The girl's face fell. Her gaze darted to the oar in the boat. She tried to grab it, to use it to save herself, but he got to it first and held the dull edge at her throat.

"Don't try to fight me, Siren. You and I are partners now. We're going to have a long, beautiful friendship. Because while you might control me through the night, I'll certainly control you through the day," he said. His free hand swung out and caught the side of her face. The girl stared at him with wide eyes as everything she knew slipped away in a heartbeat; all the names, all the places, all the thoughts and hopes, and the boy who had saved her from the river that day.

She blinked. Then she looked around, wondering where she was, why the sky was angry, and who this person standing in front of her was. A silver-haired fairy extended a hand with a smile and said, "Hello there, Siren. I'm Barnabus. Your friend."

For three and a half years the girl and Barnabus travelled across the Four Corners of Ever, performing crimes in the capitol cities and villages alike. They were nearly unstoppable, growing rich and evading every authority who tried to hunt them down to restore order. But on a chilly day after they returned to the North Corner of Ever, they picked the wrong fairy to rob, and they found themselves surrounded by a band of females with sharp weapons.

"Stand back, you faeborn females! My partner will haunt your dreams! She'll bring nightmares to your door—" Barnabus's words were cut off as he was stabbed. The girl gasped.

The remaining females surrounded the girl with fairsabers poised at her throat, and she lifted her hands in surrender.

As the girl watched her partner of over three years fade away, she felt her heart twist in her chest. It was the first thing she'd felt in a long time. Having lost all her memories, she'd found it difficult to feel anything at all most days. But perhaps losing Barnabus was something she wasn't ready for. She didn't know anyone else.

The silver-haired Shadow Fairy reached for her with his last bout of strength. He cast her a strange, unexpected smile, and as his breathing turned ragged, he whispered, "Thank you for such a fun ending to my existence. As a gift, I'll give back what I stole from you before I go, Siren."

She didn't know what he meant until he lifted a shaky hand and placed it against the side of her face.

Warmth bled through her mind.

All at once, an entire childhood of memories flashed inward, burning into her understanding like a flame. She saw a sinking ship, she saw the moment she met Barnabus for the first time, how he'd tricked her. She saw her months on the Mycra Sentorious, how her captain had mistreated her and forced her to bring nightmares and terrors upon his enemies. She saw the village where she grew up. How the crew of the Mycra Sentorious had approached and pressured her mother to sell her when the poor woman couldn't speak up to object.

The girl lifted a hand over her trembling lips as she recalled.

Barnabus choked, struggling for air. The girl watched him take his final breath, his eyelids sliding closed forever. But she felt an entirely different set of feelings about his passing now. Tears filled her eyes—the first time in over three years that had happened—and she sat there, stunned, until one of the females around her spoke.

"Is it true you have a gift?" the female asked.

The girl couldn't speak. Her throat was thick. Her mouth was dry.

"I'll give you a choice then. I can kill you alongside your friend—"

"He was not my friend," the girl rasped, realizing it far too late.

"Ah. I see. Then perhaps you'd like to take the second option. Join us, and I'll help you develop your gift. I can make you truly lethal so no Shadow Fairy can ever control you like that again," the female promised.

The girl looked up with stinging red eyes, beholding a fierce-looking fairy with black hair like hers, wild green eyes, and fair skin. It was like looking at an older version of herself.

"Not all dreamslippers look the same," the female said, "but, *queensbane*, clearly a few of us do." She put away her fairsaber and extended a hand. "You're not alone anymore, fairy. Train with us. Give me five years, and I'll turn you into a deadly and powerful thing no one will be able to stop. You'll never have to work for another soul in your faeborn life."

The girl eyed the female's hand. "Who are you?" she asked.

"We're the remnant of the Sisterhood of Assassins of the North."

"A remnant?" The girl blinked her tears away.

The female huffed a bitter laugh. "We were disbanded and mostly slaughtered by our Brotherhood counterpart. But pockets of us survived. We're attempting to rise again and wage war on the Queene."

Strength returned to the girl's legs, and she stood. "I have someone to f…" she began, but she stopped.

Once, she'd had someone to find. Someone who had promised to come back and find her. But it seemed Dranian had never tracked her down like he said he would. Not in the months she'd been on the ship, and not in the three years she'd been at Barnabus's side. If Dranian Evelry had been searching for her, he could have followed the rumours of the dreamslipper. Barnabus's tactics weren't subtle.

Did she still have someone to find? If she hunted Dranian down now, would he still want to see her? Much time had passed. Perhaps he'd forgotten about the promise he'd made. And besides… she'd promised him she would protect him. She swore to become his fairy guard. And she'd watched him get beaten with rocks and sold.

The girl swallowed and looked back at the fierce female. A dreamslipper who embodied a vision of power. Someone who could teach her to be powerful, too. Someone who could stop her from getting taken advantage of.

"My unhidden name is Rosa. What's your name?" the female asked, seeming to notice the girl's resolve change.

The girl thought about it. Barnabus had only ever called her 'Siren', but she wasn't a siren.

So, after some thought, she said, "Mycra Sentorious."

A sunken ship would never return to reclaim its name. And even though it was unlikely at this point, the girl wanted to give Dranian a way to track her down if he ever chose to. If the one name he knew was the name of the ship she'd left on, perhaps someday he would follow the name to her.

The secret training base was hidden away in an abandoned castle off the cusp of a great cliff, surrounded by thick trees and hardly visible to anyone on the outside. The Sisterhood of Assassins swung weapons at each other in various chambers, supplies lined rickety shelves, and sunlight glided in through gaping holes in the ceiling. The girl passed several small knitting groups on her way in.

"It's good for the mind," she was told when she was caught staring. "And there are tricks in yarn, you see. Ways to weave enchantments into your clothing."

The girl entered the training at a disadvantage. She had assumed she would be joining the secret Sisterhood as the only new recruit, but that was not the case. Thirty other young females, all of whom were bigger and stronger than her, began training on the same day, some clothed in expensive-looking armour. For that reason alone, the girl should have been eliminated in the first test of strength. She should have backed out willingly before she began taking hits and losing blood. But the girl had survived many masters, and for that, she decided to turn her fears into a will of iron and forge it into a blade.

She worked twice as hard as the other assassin recruits. One by one, she beat out other females in the fighting boundaries, growing her speed and especially her strength. Rosa gave her particular attention, working with her through the nights to sharpen her dreamslipping talents. Before two and a half years had passed, the Sisterhood had crafted the girl with a new name into the most dangerous, effective weapon they had. The girl was trained in body and mind. She was washed of fear and emotion. She was, in every respect, unstoppable.

She was Mycra Sentorious, the dreamslipper of the secret Sisterhood of Assassins of the North. She was the one thing the Sisterhood believed would bring down the Queene.

CHAPTER

17

Luc Zelsor and the Myth of the Mountain God

The stars were particularly shiny on the eve before the final Yule ceremony. Luc's bed was strung with walnut lights, and sugar plums rested in a bowl beside his bed, waiting for morning. Their scent was delicious and sweet—when he sniffed, he could already taste the purple fruit with the hard sugar shell on his tongue.

He gazed up at the stars, considering it a Yuletide miracle that he could see them at all, that the ever-clouds had taken a rest from their toiling for a night. Perhaps it was a gift from the sky deities who had taken pity upon a young, poorly behaved fox who sat alone most days, watching the other childlings play from afar.

A squeaking sound lifted through his room, and when he looked back, he saw his mother getting comfortable on the braidwood chair. Her hair was tangled and messy like she'd been trying to sleep up until now and was unsuccessful.

"You can't sleep, either?" Luc asked. He scrambled to the edge of his bed to be closer to her. "Is it because you're excited for the Great Yule Morning, too?"

"Actually, I thought I might whisper a Yuletide story to you, dear Luc." She smiled and pulled a thick book out from where she'd been hiding it in her nightdress. Sounds of gently flipped pages and a deep, cracking tome spine filled Luc's room as she found her spot. "This story is precious. It means something to me," she added.

Luc plopped onto his stomach, propping his cheeks up with his palms to listen. His mother's fingers were stained black with ink from painting flowers for wreaths. She was a renowned wreathweaver; the best in the Dark Corner, some had said. She'd been working extra hard these last weeks to make wreaths worthy of being placed in the throne room. The Dark Queene herself had requested she cover the thrones in the fragrance of the most prestigious blossoms of the Dark Corner.

"There once lived a young fox who faced every obstacle with cunning and determination," his mother began to read.

Luc smiled and snuggled into his bedsheets a little deeper, pleased it was a story about creatures like him.

"The fox grew to the capable age of twenty-five years and found he had reached the greatest measure of strength he ever would." His mother flipped a page, and Luc raised a brow. It seemed early to be flipping a page when the story had only just begun. "And so, on a cold Wynter's day, he began a great trek up a mountain to face the greatest obstacle of all—another fox. One twice his age, and equal in power."

"Why would he do that?" Luc asked.

"Because, in his mind, only one fox could live and rule over ordinary fairies. And twenty-five is the magical age when one must decide these sorts of things," she said.

Luc smirked. "There's no such thing as ordinary fairies," he objected. "Every fairy has power in their own way."

"Oh dear." His mother smiled. "You think like I do, Luc." Luc beamed as his mother dragged a finger down the page like she was looking for where she'd left off. She cleared her throat. "When the fox reached the top of the mountain, he entered the battle of his life. But even though he was a cunning fox, he was unprepared because he assumed himself to be greater than he was. And sometimes just because we wish to be the greatest, doesn't mean we are." Her mouth tipped down at the corners.

She continued on, explaining how the foxes fought a long and deadly battle. Only one of them survived—the fox who had climbed the mountain in the first place.

It took Luc three minutes of her flipping pages off-beat for him to realize she was not reading the story out of the book at all. She was reciting a tale she had memorized. Luc didn't know his mother had stories memorized.

"So, he won," Luc concluded. "The fox the tale is about. He

climbed a mountain and faced a foe that was more difficult than he expected, but he survived." It was a simple story, but Luc enjoyed it.

His mother nodded. "It wasn't an easy victory though. It cost him everything he had to come back down that mountain alive."

Luc thought about that. "What do you mean by *everything?*" His fingers grazed over the nine fox tails hidden beneath his nightclothes. "How many of his fox lives did it take to win?" His mother closed the book and rested it on her lap.

"All of them but one," she said, and Luc's hand tightened over his nine tails. "You should never turn your back to a fox, Luc. Even if you're a fox yourself," she said. "Remember this story so you don't forget that even foxes can turn against each other."

Luc sighed and rolled onto his back to look up at the stars again. "I don't know any other foxes, apart from Father."

He did not realize right away that his mother had gone quiet as he studied the glimmers in the heavens. One star was bigger than the others. Luc leaned forward a little to try and press the image into his memory before the clouds returned and stole it away.

"You know, some fairies say your father came down from a mountain after a great battle, too." His mother bit her lower lip. "Isn't that funny?"

Luc did not find it funny, but he offered her a smile anyway. "Is that why some fairies call him the Mountain God?" he asked. "Because he came down from a mountain just like that fox of legend in the tale?"

This time, his mother didn't seem to be joking around. "Yes," she said.

Luc sighed and gazed out at the heavens one last time, wondering if he should thank the sky deities for the small gift of stars. "I like to study the stars," he told his mother, changing the subject. "Maybe I should paint them before they go away."

"You have always been a curious childling," his mother said, her smile returning. Then she added, "You are cunning too, like your father, Luc. Perhaps you should study people instead."

A whiff of sugar plums brushed Luc's nose, stealing his focus. He gazed at those plump, syrupy fruits. How he wanted to taste one—just one bite—before he was allowed. There were so many lovely things to be distracted by tonight.

His mother's laugh reminded him he could do no such tasting until morning, lest he break the sacred tradition.

"Morning is just a few hours away, Luc," his mother said as she stood from the chair. "Try to get some sleep before then. I'm sure you'll dream of sugar plum fairies."

Two weeks after the Great Yule Morning, Luc's father returned from a long trip where rumour claimed he had engaged in the revels of the Army and had forgotten about his duties at the Shadow Palace. He had not even returned for the Great Yule Morning. Luc had been forced to eat at the Queene's dining table alone, since his father was absent and the Queene forbade his peasant mother from sitting at her table.

When his father marched into the Shadow Palace, he went straight for Luc's mother and met with her behind a closed door. That was the day Luc's parents had made a bet, and a bargain, for their son. It was the same week Luc's mother had lost him and been banished from the Palace forever.

The day after her exile, Luc found a note hiding beneath his pillow. It was a blank piece of parchment with a ripple of wetness in the corner just the size of a fallen tear. He knew how to read it—his mother had left him notes like this in the past to be silly. It was a note only his breath could unlock, and no one else's.

Luc breathed on the parchment, and a set of clear words filled the page for just a second before they dissolved again:

WHEN THE TIME COMES

KILL HIM OR RUN FROM HIM

BUT DO NOT BE RULED BY HIM

She left nothing else behind.
Nothing but Luc.

18

Mycra Sentorious

A layer of frost coated the classroom desks the day the Brotherhood of Assassins came. They swarmed the Sisterhood's training castle like bugs in navy and black-shelled skins, taking hostages and killing those who fought back. The entire resistance rang out with the sounds of fairy roars and buzzing fairsabers.

Mycra Sentorious stood stone-still as they rushed into her classroom. As they tossed over desks and dragged her sisters away. She took in the faces and movements of the males, counting their attacks, catching their habits. Finding their leader.

"Mycra! *Help!*" Quiver screamed back as the fair girl was pulled into the hall and enchanted vines were slapped onto her wrists. Quiver tried to fight—she kicked, she screamed, she bit.

Mycra calculated. She could save Quiver. She could save one or two others and help them escape. But that wouldn't stop their enemies from taking over the castle and rounding up everyone as hostages.

However...

Taking down their leader might be enough.

Mycra climbed onto the nearest desk and leapt over the feud in the hallway. She sprang off the far wall, drawing her half-spear as she came down, and driving it through a male assassin in her way. She raced toward *him*—the young, deadly-looking fae wearing the signet ring of the ward Prince. She dropped two more male bodies, sweeping down the hall like the deadly siren of the seas she claimed not to be, and she brought her spear down upon his fairsaber.

The leader looked up at her, his cold, turquoise eyes calm and focussed. He was unalarmed, even as he took her in and calculated every inch of her worth. He stabbed suddenly, and Mycra dodged. When he swung his arm toward her, she blocked and prepared a strike of her own, but she wasn't ready for the weight of faestone to knock her upside the head. Mycra slammed into the wall, going dizzy for a spell. She pushed herself up in time to see Rosa waging war upon the males at the end of the hall. It was her against three. And suddenly Mycra no longer cared for the male leader.

She spun away from the ward Prince and stabbed her way toward her mentor—barely seeing the bodies fall at her own feet.

"Rosa!" she shouted. "Hang on! I'm coming!"

She tried. With everything she had, she tried. She fought skin and bone and flesh and blood; she conquered strength and steel. But Mycra did not make it. She watched the fairsaber drive into Rosa's body. And, forgetting all the careful practice she had endured to contain her emotions since the day she joined the Sisterhood, Mycra screamed. A male assassin tore his fairsaber from Rosa, and the only other dreamslipper Mycra had ever known fell to the floor; an unmoving, beautiful body.

Time stood still. The fight around Mycra became nothing more than shifting shapes and colours. And then... it was war.

It took twelve of the male assassins to bring Mycra down— five of those she killed. They dragged her away with her sisters who had survived, only thirty in total.

A long, cold, silent day later, Mycra found herself on her knees before Queene Levress. The very Queene she'd been meant to destroy. Mycra boldly lifted her gaze to look the Queene in the eyes. She wondered if she should avenge Rosa, and the rest of her sisters, and simply finish the Queene now. She wondered how well the Queene slept at night. If she dreamt of nice things. If she was strong enough to endure nightmares.

But Queene Levress's chilled, pale smile spread like she could read Mycra's mind. Like she could feel the story coming off Mycra's burning flesh. "This one will be trouble." The Queene's high, icy voice crawled over Mycra's skin. But Mycra didn't bat an eye, even as the Queene's long silver nails reached toward her and took her chin.

Mycra stared back at her dully. Nothing could scare her any-more. She'd already lost everything. Several times.

"Give her to me as a gift, Your Majesty." A fairy of some im-portance lounged across a modest throne that wasn't nearly as lovely as the great thrones at the head of the room. His pure white hair and wide smile didn't dilute the devilish look in his eye. "If you don't want the trouble, that is. I'll take her as a gift for my heir."

Mycra finally tore her eyes from the Queene of the North Cor-ner and settled them on the middle-aged Lord. He wore a long crimson robe with a crest carefully stitched over his chest in ex-pensive thread. When he stood, his robe unrolled, revealing a name amidst the artwork: LYRO.

Lyro…

Lyro. She'd heard that name before. Back in the village—the same day Dranian Evelry was sold.

Mycra's gaze shot back to the Queene to see what she would do.

"If you wish. I don't need any more powerful slaves." Queene Levress flicked her hand, passing Mycra off without care.

"Queensbane," Mycra whispered, biting down on the word. It was the first thing she'd said since entering the Silver Castle. But she could hardly believe her fate. Could hardly believe her years of trouble had led her here.

She was going to the House of Lyro where Dranian Evelry—

the quiet boy who'd saved her in the river—was sent all those years ago.

Mycra was optimistic when she arrived, her gaze searching every court and patio as she was dragged through a great set of red-painted gates. She walked behind a crossbeast carrying the High Lord of the Lyro House, enchanted vines tightly binding her wrists. Servants crowded around her, and Mycra strained to see through them. They passed a tall pagoda of many levels, came across a glass-floored courtyard with a great crystal fountain in the middle, and entered an enormous mansion half as large as the Silver Castle.

She looked for Dranian Evelry everywhere. She looked for him day and night, even after she was shoved into a large golden cage meant to be her living quarters. She didn't dare speak to the nobles, but she asked one of the servants about him the next day. "Is there a fairy guard here by the name of Dranian Evelry, by chance?"

The servant raised a brow at the question, studying Mycra through the thick golden bars. "There was," she said, "but he left."

Mycra's soul dropped to the floor. "He... *left?*"

"Yes. The heir original got kicked out of the house and sent to the Silver Castle a while back. His fairy guard followed him. I think they've joined the Brotherhood of Assassins now. At least, that's the rumour the young Lords of Lyro have been laughing about these last months—that the heir original is now a slave of the Queene."

Mycra stared. Even when the servant left, she continued to stare at the same place the servant had been. She could hardly convince herself to keep taking breaths.

Dranian had been at the Silver Castle, where she *just* was.

He was a member of the Brotherhood of Assassins who had just attacked and killed so many of her sisters. He might have been there. He might have passed by her. He might have seen her and not known who she was. Oh, sky deities, what if he was one of the ones she'd killed during her capture?

Mycra's hand slowly lifted to her dull, thudding heart. She'd missed Dranian at the raid of the Sisterhood's training place. She'd missed him at the Silver Castle. She'd missed him here.

In the fifth year of Mycra's confinement at the House of Lyro, she was sitting in her golden cage, plucking the petals off a fresh flower, waiting around for something exciting to happen. There had been chaos upstairs the last few days—yelling and fighting. Something was going on at the House of Lyro. She was relieved it didn't involve her this time.

Mycra tossed the petals to the floor and pulled up her silk pillow to lean her head back against the bars. Everything in her cage was perfectly neat, stunningly beautiful, and very rich. They treated her like a queene. If only the Lyros didn't imprison their queenes behind gold bars.

She'd heard all the rumours over the past year from her confined perch. The residents of the great house seemed to forget she was there when they walked by, talking loudly. It was a skill she was relieved she still possessed from her childling years—to be invisible.

There was talk that the Prince of the North Corner had vanished. Presumed to be dead. That the Brotherhood of Assassins had gone into turmoil trying to replace their former leader. Princess Haven was betrothed a new fairy now—Lord Bonswick of the East. Their wedding would be taking place soon since the year of planning was finally coming to an end.

It was all boring.

A handful of fairies flooded into the basement. The tension in the air was thick, but there was a new fairy with them Mycra had not seen before. He had white hair like the Lyro family, but his overall presence was different. While the Lyro fairies had clean faces and pure bodies, this new fairy had small scars over his shoulders, a few scattered tattoos, and fingers that looked as though they'd been broken then melded back together like he'd been in battle. It made Mycra curious.

The new fairy looked around as if recalling old memories, and his pretty blue gaze fell on her. A wide smile broke out across his face, and he moseyed over to her cage. Mycra lazily lifted from her plush bed and stretched, deciding she'd take a nap soon. But she came to the bars to meet him because her curiosity got the best of her. He was handsome too, but that didn't move her much.

"Queensbane, who exactly are *you*?" he asked in an amused voice.

She glanced down at his bare feet. "I'm a weapon. Don't get too close; I bite," she whispered with ample threat, and his smile widened.

"How delightful," he said. Then he glanced up and around at her bars, seeming to question their sturdiness. "Can I interest you in a kiss, pretty fairy?" he offered, taking hold of two bars and shaking them a little. They didn't budge an inch.

Mycra laughed. "You must wish to enchant me and turn me against my masters. You'll be killed on the spot if you try."

"I *am* one of your masters," the fairy promised with a twinkle in his eye, and Mycra's face changed as she thought about that. She knew all the masters of this house but one. That meant he had to be…

"I'm Shayne." He reached a hand through the bars for a handshake, and Mycra blanched. "I think we may get along well here," he added.

Lord Shayne Lyro, former heir to the House of Lyro. Returned after five long years.

He would be dead by sunrise.

And he'd asked her for a kiss. Was he insane?

"Don't you know who I am?" she asked, taking a small step

back from the bars. "Don't you realize we've already met?"

Shayne didn't bat an eye when he said, "I imagine you're the dreamslipper who's been haunting my nights, calling me home."

Mycra's smile was long gone. She could never smile about the nightmares. She rarely came face-to-face with the victims of them. And this was no ordinary victim. This was a fairy who was in close vicinity of another fairy she once knew.

"Is your fairy guard here?" Mycra asked before she could remember to hold her secrets close.

Shayne's face changed. "My fairy guard? No. I left that grumpy latte addict at home," he said without missing a beat. He studied Mycra as her shoulders dropped. "But I'm dying to know why you're interested in *my* Dranian," he added, appearing a smidgen wary.

Mycra swallowed and collected herself. "Never mind," she whispered. She stood a little taller and took the hand Shayne still extended through the bars, waiting.

"You shouldn't associate with me unless you want trouble, Lord Lyro," she warned him, and his smile grew. She cocked her head, looking him up and down, calculating his strength, his stability, how he might perform in a fight. How easy it might be to kill him and escape if she had to—just for curiosity's sake. "But I agree. I think we may get along quite well."

CHPTER

· ⟫⟩⟩⟩⟩⟩⟩⟩ · ⟨⟨⟨⟨⟨⟨⟨⟨ ·

19

Dranian Evelry and the Present Issue of Never Sleep

Coffee was not enough. Dranian spent the whole evening rest-lessly trying to distract himself so he wouldn't fall asleep. He spent most of the time in his bedroom pacing. Finally, he went to the kitchen and nibbled on cookies, he did stretches, he played fetch with Dog-Shayne until Dog-Shayne fell back to sleep. He finally caved and called Cress in the twilight hours.

"What in the faeborn-cursed human realm are you calling me for at this hour?! I thought once Shayne left I'd finally get some sleep!" Cress's loud complaints came through the phone before any kind of greeting.

"I can't come into work today," Dranian stated.

"Why ever not?" Cress asked through a yawn.

"I've avoided slumber all night. I'm ill." Dranian waited for the verdict.

After a few seconds, Cress released a growly moan. But then he said, "Fine. Get better."

Dranian laid back on the couch and thought that over. It was clear Cress hadn't a clue Shayne had snuck off. Apparently, Lily hadn't told anyone about what she'd discovered from her phone call to Greyson.

So, Dranian called Lily next.

"What's wrong?!" Her voice was panicked, desperate, and raspy from sleep. "What happened, Dranian?!"

Dranian made a face. "Nothing faeborn happened," he said dully.

Lily let out a breath of relief. "Then why are you calling me at four a.m.? I thought that fox-guy was murdering you or something!"

"You didn't tell anyone that Shayne lied," Dranian said. "I thought you would have told them."

Lily paused. "I thought *you* would have told them."

"That's nonsense. You're at the café more than me. I only work there part time now," Dranian countered.

"I only work there part time, too. Seriously Dranian, I've always been part time."

Another pause.

"Right." Dranian nodded.

"And to be honest," Lily's fidgeting was practically coming

through the phone, "I didn't want to say anything until I knew why Shayne lied to us."

Dranian tapped his chin in thought. "You think we shouldn't tell the others?" He hated the thought of hiding something *else* from his High Court. One secret was enough for him—two would be positively torturous.

"I think they'll find out as soon as Kate has a conversation with Greyson. But for now, I just want to figure out what's going on. I've texted Shayne like thirty times, and he hasn't replied," she said.

"His phone is with me. He didn't take it," Dranian told her. He stood from the couch to pace, wondering if he should make more coffee to keep himself awake. "Why don't we give Shayne three days?" Dranian had to save Dog-Shayne in the next three days anyway. "If he doesn't turn up, then we'll hunt for him," he finished.

Lily's heavy sigh came through the phone. "I hate keeping secrets from Kate."

"I hate keeping secrets from Cress and Mor," Dranian returned. He glanced at the floor. "But if it was me, and Shayne found out I had lied, he wouldn't dare oust me before the others until he knew why I did it."

"Yeah."

A third pause went by.

"We'll reconvene in three days' time," Dranian mumbled in decision. "Hopefully Shayne comes back on his own before then."

"I can live with that," Lily said. "Talk to you later. Watch your back."

Dranian hung up the phone and went to the kitchen for more cookies. He'd just stuffed a large one into his mouth when his phone rang again. He answered horribly with his mouth full. "Heh-wow?"

"Are you sneaking night snacks?" Mor's voice filled his ear. Dranian forced himself to swallow the cookie, his throat suddenly feeling dry. "Yes," he confessed. It was one thing he *could* confess.

"Cress just woke me from a deep sleep with a *phone call* and told me you haven't been sleeping. That you can't even come into work. He's asking me to fill in for you," Mor said.

Dranian swatted crumbs off his lips. "My apologies," he said, glancing at the clock. How typical of Cress to call Mor at such an hour over a shift placement.

"That's not why I'm calling. I don't mind working at the café. I'm wondering why you can't sleep."

A creak sounded in the background, and Dranian pictured Mor walking around his big, ugly, creaky cathedral.

Dranian found himself pacing again.

"I… I accidentally replied to a dreamslipper," Dranian admitted, reaching the end of the living space. When he turned around, he froze in place.

Luc stood there. Staring at him.

"Queensbane, Dranian. What would possess you to speak to a

faeborn dreamslipper?" Mor asked. "Do you want me to mix you a sleep remedy to keep it out?"

Dranian nearly threw the phone out the window. "Mor," he said, "I'll have to call you back." Dranian slammed the "end call" button. He dropped his phone to the couch like it was a hot coal. Then he eyed Luc. "Did you hear all that?" he asked, balling his fists at his sides.

"Unfortunately." Luc sounded uninterested, but he couldn't hide a teensy tiny smirk that tugged at the corner of his mouth. He turned around, but not before Dranian saw it. "I once responded to a dreamslipper in my childling years. It took me six days to kick her out of my head," he said.

"Six days?" Dranian gaped. He'd never heard of someone escaping the clutches of a dreamslipper so fast. "One of my allies in the Brotherhood tried for six months to get his dreams back."

Luc glanced over at him. "What do you mean, *tried*?"

Dranian closed his mouth, deciding not to explain that the fairy had gone mad and tossed himself into the Jade Ocean after never succeeding. But by the look on Luc's face, it seemed the fox could figure out the end of the story on his own.

A female scream came from the hall, and Dranian's skin tightened. It had sounded like Beth.

Luc sighed and swung the apartment door open, revealing Beth standing outside in the dark hall with a pale face. She stared down in horror at a fairy bound tightly by vines and rope, squirming on the ground in the middle of the hall.

"Oh dear," Luc said. "Hold still for me, will you dear Beth?" He reached over and grabbed her forehead with one hand while rolling and kicking the fairy through the door into 3E with his foot. Dranian's eyes widened as he recognized the Shadow Fairy that had put the wristlet onto Dog-Shayne in Luc's memory—the one fairy in existence who therefore had the power to remove it. Dranian grabbed the fool's foot and dragged him the rest of the way in, out of Beth's sight.

Luc dropped his hand from Beth's forehead. The human female gasped and looked straight ahead, all her screaming forgotten. She blinked. Then she looked around. Looked down at her human pajamas. "What just happened? I literally can't remember what I was just saying. Why did I come out here, again?" she asked.

Luc shrugged and brushed some invisible thing off his sleeves. "Beats me. Have a nice day." He stepped into the apartment and closed the door behind him. Then he nudged the Shadow Fairy with his foot.

From the floor, the Shadow Fairy gaped at the apartment, taking in the folded blankets on the couch, the TV, the curtains. Dranian.

"I brought a gift for Dog-Shayne. As much as I enjoyed watching him fight, I never should have bound his fate to mine. So, now he'll be free, and we can keep the rest of it between us fairies," he said.

The fox whistled and the sound of Dog-Shayne lifting from his dog bed came from the kitchen. As soon as the dog appeared and padded over, Luc put his heel against the Shadow Fairy's neck. "Remove the blossoms from this mutt," he demanded.

The Shadow Fairy glared up at Luc. "You'll be killed for this."

"Oh dear. I'm already going to die; did you forget?" Luc flashed him a smile and shook his wrist in the air to rattle his branch wristlet. "Now, remove the blossom you placed on this mutt, or I'll crush your windpipe."

"You just tossed away your last two days alive by snatching me, Zelsor! The Army will come claim you immediately once they realize—" The Shadow Fairy's face blanched as Luc drew his fairsaber. The saber moved provocatively close to the fairy's neck as Luc brought it down to slice the vines and ropes. As soon as the Shadow was free of his binds, he scrambled back against the wall. "Airslip, and I'll chase you to your death," Luc warned. Then he nodded back to Dog-Shayne. "Free the mutt."

The Shadow Fairy looked at the dog, a stroke of fear crossing his silver-brown eyes. He reached for Dog-Shayne's wristlet, snapped the branches in half, and quickly yanked his hand back to himself. The whole wristlet fell to the floor, shrivelling into ashy bits of dried flowers and dust.

"You're a lunatic, Zelsor," the Shadow Fairy said. "You can't possibly take on the whole Shadow Army by yourself."

The claim hung in the air as a broad, twisted smile crossed Luc's beautiful face. "Watch me, you fool."

The Shadow Fairy snarled. Then, as Luc had forbade him from

doing, he vanished.

Luc sighed. He cursed. He scratched his head. "I did warn him," he said, bracing to airslip, but Dranian stopped him with a growl.

"*Don't* let him get away! That fool tried to kill my dog!" he said, then asked, "What will you do to him?"

Luc thought about it. "I think I'll make him too weak to airslip and drop him from the sky. How does that sound?" he decided. "Don't worry, North Fairy. I'll cover my tracks. I'm good at that." Luc paused for a moment, and Dranian got a strange feeling about the look that came over the fox's face. "Farewell, North Fairy. I know we're not allies by any measure of the word, but I appreciated not being alone for a little while."

There was a pause. A single heartbeat. Dranian didn't have time to ask the question that hung in the air.

Luc disappeared—a slip of colour turning to dust—and Dranian was left there with a freshly freed Dog-Shayne.

The apartment seemed strangely empty and quiet all of a sudden. Dranian stared at the spot where Luc had been. Something felt off, like there was an obvious sign in the sky and he was missing it. He turned all the way around, trying to sniff out the oddity. As he did, he realized for the first time that Luc's spare pair of shoes were missing from the matt by the door. All his crumbs had been cleaned from the living room, too.

Dranian went to Luc's bedroom and peeked inside.

A strange feeling found him at the sight of Luc's bed made.

The fox's satchel of belongings wasn't anywhere in sight. He rushed into the bathroom next, and lo and behold, Luc's toothbrush was gone.

Dranian came out with the realization that he was the victor after all. *Him.* Luc had packed up his things and run for his faeborn life. And if the nine tailed fox wasn't coming back, Dranian could joyfully revel in the rewards of having his apartment all to himself again.

That was what he wanted.

He scratched his temple.

This had to be a trick.

Was the fool really not coming back? Was this a fox ruse to get Dranian's hopes up? Had Dranian really conquered a legendary nine tailed fox all on his own?

He headed for the window and looked out. The sky was clear of airslippers, and a huff of disbelief escaped him. It was real. Luc was gone.

Finally, Dranian could go before his brothers and tell them all that had happened. He could announce that he had handled it himself and that, should danger ever come his way again, he would be just fine—damaged arm or not.

It would have been an adequate time to smile, but for whatever reason a smile never came. Dranian studied the living room, wondering if it had always been so big. If there had always been so much extra air and space everywhere. A light chill moved through the empty apartment, and Dranian shuddered. He went to Dog-

Shayne's side.

Now that it was just the two of them, Dranian turned to his pet and said, "I demand you barf up that thistle."

Dog-Shayne blinked at him with all the innocence and adoration of a true, reliable ally. And so, Dranian decided to let it go. He was feeling tired anyway. He stood and stretched, thinking about going to the grocery store for pasta noodles now that Dog-Shayne's safety was no longer a concern. Perhaps Dog-Shayne could carry some of the groceries home.

But Dranian's eyes burned from lack of sleep, his body wanted to fall to the floor, and every particle of his being wanted to rest. He wouldn't make it to the grocery store in this state, even when morning came. With a sigh, he decided he would sit on the couch and allow his eyes to close for a second—just to relieve the sting.

"Dranian."

He stood face-to-face with a bright-eyed female. He nearly jumped out of his skin—he tried to fall backwards, to wake himself from this dream, but she latched onto his arm with a force that didn't feel at all natural.

"Your friend is here where I am," she said, like before. Only this time, she added, *"Shayne Lyro."*

Dranian halted his escape.

How did she know that name?

Lily's words rang in Dranian's ears from when she'd discovered Shayne wasn't in the kingdom of Florida like he'd told everyone. It was too much of a coincidence to believe. In fact, it was so absurd, Dranian couldn't even imagine it. That Shayne had found himself in the company of a real dreamslipper.

Something doubled over in Dranian's chest—but he could not be fooled this easily. He swallowed, drawing in caution, every breath a risk.

"Who are you?" he asked the female. Speaking to a dreamslipper only gave them more control, but looking at this fairy now, it didn't seem like control was what she was after. In fact... Dranian slammed his eyes shut, refusing to acknowledge what his mind might have been telling him all along.

That she was familiar.

"I think you know who I am. I can tell you remember me. Snap out of it and listen! Do you know how hard it was to find you like this? And now you won't even hear what I have to say?!" she said with a tone of accusation.

Dranian inhaled deeply as he remembered that girl with no name from the village. The one who could slip into dreams. The one he had watched slay a hogbeast with just a half-spear. The one who had sunk to the bottom of the Twilight Lakes.

"You're dead," he said back. "That's how I know this is a trick."

Shock crossed the girl's face. She stared at him for several passing heartbeats, her lips parted, her eyes widening. *"You thought…"*

"Queensbane, get out of my head, you ghost!" Dranian roared, and she took a staggered step back. Wind and rain formed in the space around them, mimicking the torment in Dranian's soul. It blew at his clothes; it tousled her black hair.

When she spoke again, it was quieter this time. *"I know you have no reason to believe a dreamslipper. I know you think you can't trust a word I say because I could have stolen any of this information from your dreams. But Shayne Lyro is going to die,"* she said. *"He said you and him were the best of friends. That's why I've been trying to find you."*

"Why should I believe that?" Dranian looked around his dream now, wondering if a cliff would form so he could hop from it, or a lake which he could fall into. Something that would startle him awake.

"He called you a grumpy latte addict," she said, and Dranian's eyes slowly drifted back to her. Dreams were strange things— maybe he had heard her incorrectly.

"What did you just say?" he asked anyway.

"He called you a grumpy. Latte. Addict," she articulated. *"He doesn't even know I'm reaching out to you. He didn't want you here. But he cares about you, I can tell. So, I found you anyway."* She set her jaw. *"I have no reason to help either of you. You never came back for me like you said you would. But you saved my life once. So, I'm returning the favour."*

Dranian slapped a fist over his mouth. It was possibly the most expression he'd ever mustered on one occasion. But that information she spoke of had not been anywhere near the forefront of his mind all these years. It would not have been easy for a dreamslipper to access knowledge like that if he'd never dreamt about it. So, either this was the most powerful dreamslipper he had ever heard about, or…

Or this really was her. That girl. The one with no name.

And she really was with Shayne.

"Where are you?" he demanded, dropping his hand and stepping in. His faeborn heart began to pound. He needed to get to Shayne. To her.

She looked between his eyes like she was trying to gauge if he truly believed her now. Then finally, she said, *"I'm at the House of Lyro."*

Dranian's mouth slammed shut.

No.

No, Shayne could not possibly be there. He was supposed to be on vacation. He should be somewhere in the human realm still, lying on a beach, not back in the Ever Corners. Not…

Queensbane, Shayne was going to die.

"I'm going to—Gah!" A stabbing pain burst through Dranian's side, stealing his words. His rhythms took off, his eyesight wavered. His whole dream shook. The stabbing came again, and he nearly buckled forward.

The girl looked around, worry etching over her features. *"Dranian,"* she said. Then she grabbed his shoulders and shouted it louder. *"Dranian! You need to wake up now!"*

"Are you doing this?" he demanded, feeling the nightmare sink in.

Her face changed. The girl's hands slid off his shoulders and she took a step back, appearing dumbfounded.

Dranian's body was struck by something, and he fell to the side. He wheezed, and he gritted his teeth.

"Dranian! This isn't a nightmare! Someone is hurting you outside of your dream! WAKE UP!" She growled it—demanded it— *threatened* it, even.

The next hit ripped him from his slumber.

Dranian's eyes opened just in time to see a fist coming for his face. He rolled off the couch, hitting the floor with a thud. Two hands grabbed and hoisted him up, and Dog-Shayne barked in protest until one of the fairies kicked him into the bedroom and shut the door.

Dranian wanted to shout, *"Don't touch my dog!"* but as his eyes fell upon the fairy he was face-to-face with, a fairy he only recognized from a mostly black and white dream, all his words grew too heavy in his mouth to say aloud.

The Dark Prince's long, scarlet hair was even more vibrant in person. He glowered at Dranian. Then he said, "Take him."

CHAPTER

20

Dranian Evelry and the Madness of War Fae

Lightning heated the sky even though it wasn't raining. Dull, gray air soaked the streets with humidity, and Dranian peeled his eyes open. Strands of his wet, auburn hair blocked his vision, chopping his view of wolf-like Shadow Fairies armoured in black pearl with death on their fingertips. They were a pack too large to imagine, swarming an abandoned park—possibly cleared of living souls on purpose.

A terrible, sharp ache burned up Dranian's shoulder. He gasped, realizing his arms were being restrained roughly behind his back. His useless arm *could not* twist that way—warm tears sprang into his eyes from the strain.

He was on his knees. Before him stood the High Prince of the Dark Corner.

"It seems my son captured and killed one of my war fairies. Now he's fled somewhere far away." Reval Zelsor's voice was dark and alluring, like a black cavern with a beast inside that called to those passing by. It made Dranian's insides tighten as the Dark Prince's words sank in.

Luc captured and killed a Shadow Fairy?

Yes. Yes, he did, Dranian realized. The fairy that had bound Dog-Shayne to a wristlet. But where was Luc now? Dranian looked right and left, seeing only enemy fairies marked by iridescent black.

Of course Luc wasn't here though. His toothbrush had been missing.

Dranian's eyes slid closed as it dawned on him what was happening. That Luc had left forever—fled to save himself before his three days were up. And now Dranian would deal with the consequences in his absence. What a horrid parting gift from his former roommate.

Dranian growled to himself, making Reval Zelsor lift a scarlet brow.

"What is the relationship between you and my son, exactly?" Reval asked. Honey and warmth bled into the air when the older fox spoke. It muffled Dranian's thoughts, and he shook the voice's lingering affects from his head. "You dwell together, but do you like or hate each other? Because this will go very poorly for you if he does not show up to save you," Reval added, slow and articulate.

"He will not come for me. Your trap is in vain," Dranian muttered.

Reval's long hair fluttered in the rising wind. His mouth twisted to the side as though thinking about that. "We'll see."

Fairsaber handles came down upon Dranian's shoulders, four at once. The ones on his right side felt dull and annoying, but the ones striking his left... His breath caught in his throat; his eyes began rapid blinking. He could hardly breathe.

He had not known pain like this in years. He might have screamed—his thoughts swirling, chasing each other, falling off the ledge of his teetering mind. Things he'd forgotten came back; old memories. Fresh ones. If he died now, he would not be able to stop the House of Lyro from killing Shayne. He would never see the girl with no name again after all these years. He would leave Dog-Shayne alone in the apartment, waiting forever for a master who would not return.

No, he could not die. Not yet. Though his mind spun, he had to fight.

Dranian dragged his hot, stinging gaze up to the Dark Prince. "He will not come!" he shouted. "Luc Zelsor is heartless and cruel. He does not know how to be kind!" Reval's eyes narrowed, but Dranian went on, "And you're breaking the bargain made between my High King and this Army division's leader—"

"The division leaders answer to me. And I did not make that

bargain," Reval stated. "I would have honoured it, however, if you had not aided in my son's betrayal. But you housed him, fed him, and *took care* of him..."

Reval paused, his words falling off into a gale. He sniffed the air. Shadows began searching the skies, but even with his acute sense of smell, Dranian was too agonized to try and pick up the scents in the wind.

"It was more like the other way around, actually." A sweet, sugary voice came from the back of the Army. Fairies looked around and parted, making a wide path right to the back.

There stood Luc.

"Oh dear. Did you really think that three-legged mutt was taking care of me? You fools." Luc's dandelion-speckled coat flapped in the wind. His hood was up, but his gaze was still visible—not sharp or deadly as it usually was. He didn't cast Reval a look, either. He studied how Dranian was on his knees, his arms twisted back, Army fairsabers poised above his shoulders ready to strike again.

Shadow Fairies whispered as Reval Zelsor slowly drew a pair of black fairsabers and began moving toward the new fox in the crowd.

Luc finally tore his gaze off Dranian and settled it on the Dark Prince coming his way.

"This is beneath you, Father. A group beating? You should challenge your foes one on one, or else you look like a coward." Luc drew his own fairsabers, and a few Army fairies gasped.

Reval came to halt. His jaw slid to the side as he contemplated. Finally, he told his warriors, "Grab him, and hold him still."

Luc raised a fairsaber toward the first fairy that stepped in his direction. "I'm here now. So let the broken North Fairy be on his way before you awaken the wrath of his brothers."

A terrifying smile spread across Reval's mouth. He wandered back to where Dranian was. "I think I'll keep him and finish what I was doing," he decided. Dranian's arms were yanked forward, and a metal bloodlock was clasped over his wrists. Reval sliced his palm open and slapped his hand onto the lock, enchanting the metal to obey only his blood.

Luc remained where he was, but his jaw tightened a little. He looked off and closed his eyes, seemingly in disbelief.

"However," Reval's cold voice flittered back to Luc, "if you want to stop me, perhaps you should stand in my way."

Reval raised the blade of his fairsaber over Dranian's neck, and Dranian felt his fight drain away, his mind closing, his hands beginning to tremble in the metal binds. He was scarcely aware when Reval's blade came down.

But the ringing of clashing metal filled his ears, startling him back to the present where the hem of Luc's black coat brushed Dranian's fingers. Luc glanced back over his shoulder at Dranian, annoyance strewn over his face. But there was another expression there—worry. Just an etch. "Breathe in and out, you fool. How could you already forget?" His words were quiet, just loud enough for Dranian's fairy ears.

Dranian sucked in a lungful and released a shuddering breath. He pulled another in, let another out. He blinked, the hazy surroundings sharpening to something he could understand.

There Luc stood, in the middle of the Shadow Army. In front of him.

"You were right about me." Luc turned back to his father. "I planned to betray you once I was of age."

Reval's face turned cold. Shadows backed away a little, giving them both space. It was as though the wind had changed directions.

But Luc went on in a tantalizing whisper, "We're less than a year away from our appointment on the mountain, aren't we?" he asked. And then, "Fight me, Father," he said. "Let's see who's the more cunning fox."

The Dark Prince reached into his pocket and pulled out a glistening red gem. He studied it. "I have a better idea. How about some sport?" He rolled the gem over his fingers.

"Stop deflecting. It makes me think you're afraid of me," Luc stated, rotating his left fairsaber and stretching his wrists. He crouched into a defensive stance.

"What do the humans call it here again? A *goalie*?" Reval asked the fairies by him. The Prince's gaze flickered up with a mark of anticipation. "I'll try to kill the North Fairy while he sits there. Block me, if you can. He takes the punishment for whatever you can't stop."

Luc seemed too annoyed to respond now. His fist tightened

subtly around his weapon. He looked like he was about to reply, but someone else spoke faster:

"How about a trade first?" A new voice—deep and filled with memories—lifted over the park, and Dranian's thoughts came to a halt. He assumed it was a delusion of his panic spell, but when he looked through a crack in the Shadow Army's formation, he knew he wasn't imagining it.

Mor.

The fairy's jean jacket eclipsed a loose white shirt flapping in the wind, and his curly hair was pulled back into a bun. Mor looked from Shadow Fairy to Shadow Fairy, then back to Dranian.

Dranian wasn't sure if he wanted to cry in relief or scream at his friend to not come any closer.

CHAPTER

21

Mor Trisencor and the Fishy Smell

Two Hours Ago

The timing was the least suspicious thing about Dranian's phone call. It wasn't exactly the fairy's tone—more like a deep sense of panic seeping through his conversation. Mor should have gone back to bed, but he sat in his office, tapping a pencil against the top of the desk. Of all the fairies, Dranian was the last one Mor wanted to be feeling *panic*.

Mor had learned the hard way that dealing with things alone only made matters worse. And Cress hadn't let him forget it. Every once in a while, Cress made sure to mention, *"that time he saved Mor from the humiliation of being defeated by his old foe,"* even though *"that time"* was not that long ago.

But now, Dranian was hiding something. And truthfully, Mor couldn't take it.

First Lily, now Dranian?

And even him.

Had the entire High Court turned into a band of teenage gossip queenes?

A yawn stole him from his thoughts. Violet came in, dragging her feet over the floor in his/Kate's fluffy slippers. She plunked into Jase's desk chair. "Why are you still up?" The human looked half asleep as she waited for an answer. He could have asked her why *she* was still here. It was almost the morning hours, and she was still working instead of sleeping at home in her comfortable bed.

Mor chose his words carefully. "I think…" He adjusted himself in his seat and reassessed how to ask. "Do you think it's possible for everyone in a close-knit group to be hiding something from each other?"

Violet blinked as though she didn't register what he'd said, and he huffed.

"Are you sleeping with your eyes open?" he accused in a dull voice. "Go home, Violet. You're the one always preaching that you need your beauty sleep—"

"You *are* all hiding something," she said. "It's super obvious."

Mor frowned. He leaned back in his chair and folded his arms. "I'm not hiding anything."

Violet was too pretty when she smiled. It was both adorable

and annoying.

"Yes, you are, Mor. You're hiding something. Lily is hiding something. Dranian is hiding something. The only one not hiding something around here is Cress, and that's because he's a blabber mouth—"

"What is Dranian hiding? Wait—" Mor shook his head. "—what is *Lily* hiding? Do you know?!"

Violet shrugged. "I have no idea." She reached over and dragged her journal from the shelf. "But the reason you all haven't caught on to each other yet is probably because you're each focussed on the thing *you're* hiding."

Mor blinked. "Are you..." He studied her journal, then her. "...*reporting* on us?"

Violet laughed like he was being absurd. She quickly slapped the journal shut and slid it back onto the shelf where it belonged. But Mor wasn't convinced. When she noticed his unbelieving face, Violet stretched her arms and completely faked another yawn.

"You're right, I should head home and go to bed." She patted a hand over her not-really-yawning mouth. "I'll see you in the morning." Violet Miller transformed into her former escape-artist-self as she left the room just as quickly as she'd arrived.

Mor sighed began tapping the pencil again.

"Oh, and if you want a really fast, really easy way to solve this problem—" Violet stuck her head back into the office, making Mor jump. "—then just get everyone together and oust them all at once. That'll get everyone talking." She flashed another pretty smile and disappeared again.

Mor tossed the pencil down. He felt like cleaning, even though the cathedral was spotless. He felt like doing *something*.

"Oh—" Mor leapt out of his chair when Violet popped back this time, his hand flying to his pounding faeborn heart. "—but go easy on Lily. I think she has more than one secret." Violet snorted a laugh.

"Leave or stay, Violet. Pick one," Mor said calmly through his teeth. His nerves couldn't take it.

Violet lifted a hand in apology and took off down the hall, her slippers slapping the hardwood the whole way.

Mor's face changed and he leapt for the doorway. "Wait!" he whispered after her in his low voice. He wasn't sure if everyone had gone home, or if Remi or Jase had fallen asleep on the furniture in the living space. Violet was already halfway down the emerald carpet, but he called after her anyway: "Queensbane, what do you mean about Lily hiding more than one thing? Violet? Violet?" He cleared his throat and tried again, "*Violet?*"

Violet waved back at him as she slipped out of sight, and Mor exhaled. He turned back and eyed her journal on the shelf. She wouldn't be offended if he flipped through it a little, would she?

As outrageous as Violet's idea was, Mor had to admit, it would probably work. If he dragged his brothers and their humans together, they could have all this sorted out in one evening. Shayne would have to come home, but it would be worth it to have everything set right. Maybe he could get Cress to plan a party.

Mor shook the last idea from his mind. If he brought Cress in on this plan, Cress would probably secretly poison a batch of cherry turnovers, make everyone eat them, and then only give the antidote to whoever confessed all their secrets.

Still.

Mor walked around his desk and lifted his jean jacket from the back of the chair. The first order of business was to deal with Dranian. The fairy wouldn't get a wink of restful sleep while tangled with a dreamslipper. Perhaps Mor could dive into his dream-memories and find a way to remedy the problem.

Mor arrived inside Dranian's apartment to find a smell he didn't expect covering the couch, left in small spaces around the kitchen, and all over the coffee machine. Mor sniffed the coffee filters, certain he had to be wrong about what his faeborn gut was saying. It all carried the smell of a familiar soul. Something like…

He laughed at the absurd thought—then he sneezed. And he winced.

There also seemed to be traces of a wet human realm animal *everywhere.*

Mor headed through the rest of Dranian's empty home, his mouth tugging down at the corners. Every step left him with a stronger indication that a struggle had taken place.

Queensbane, where was the auburn-haired fairy?

Mor went into the spare bedroom and gasped, overwhelmed by a *very* specific fox scent that had no business being there. Unease muddled his senses, a string of warnings going off in his mind. He went into Dranian's bedroom next, jumping in surprise to find an animal inside. The creature began to bark. Past it, Mor saw neatly spread bedsheets and a clean duvet. Like it hadn't been touched in a while.

The animal sprang from the bedroom and raced into the living space. Mor followed it in question, and as soon as he came around the couch, his heart seized.

Light speckles of purple fairy blood covered the floor.

"What in the faeborn-cursed human realm happened to you, Dranian?" he asked the empty apartment as he raced back out, into the hall, and down the stairs. He had his phone to his ear, ready to call Cress as he flung the entrance doors open, but he felt something move overhead. High in the sky and mixed in with the clouds. He pushed out of the apartment building and looked up.

The clouds were strange. They weren't rain clouds, but they carried gossip of shadowy mischief. Of nearby magic and mayhem. A flash of lightning erupted across the sky, and Mor nearly dropped his phone. It rang and rang for Cress, but Mor forgot about it as he picked up a thin string of scent wrapped into the wind. He followed it, clicking off his phone and shoving it back into his pocket.

Why were there traces of Shadow Fairies this far out of town?

Why did he smell a nine tailed fox in Dranian's apartment?

Where was his brother?

Mor jumped into the air and searched high and far. He scoured building tops, alleys, and the nearest park.

He found him. Beneath the eyes of the sky deities, Mor found Dranian.

Mor dropped behind a tree, his faeborn fairy blood running cold at the sight of Dranian on his knees, surrounded by the Shadow Army Mor was never supposed to have to deal with again. But mostly, what curled Mor's insides was a face he knew—one that still turned up in bad dreams on cold evenings. The face of Prince Reval; the fairy who had destroyed so much of Mor's life.

High Prince Reval stood over Dranian with a look in his eyes Mor hated to recognize; the look of a fox about to kill.

Mor gripped the tree, ripping off a handful of bark by accident. His mind waged war. Half his heart screamed at him to charge in and save his brother. The other half warned that if he did, Violet would be the one to pay the price, like before. Reval would not let anyone Mor cared about live if he presented himself now.

He padded his pocket for his phone again, but Prince Reval's sweet, cold voice made Mor slow his movements. "What is the relationship between you and my son, exactly? You dwell together, but do you like or hate each other? Because this will go very poorly for you if he does not show up to save you."

Mor's gaze shot to Dranian.

Dwell? Luc and Dranian were… *dwelling*? Mor looked off as he thought of the potent fox scent in the apartment's spare room. Had Luc been holding Dranian hostage all this time? Threatening him to keep him quiet? Tormenting him day and night?

Mor would kill Luc. It was settled.

"He will not come for me. Your trap is in vain," Dranian murmured in reply.

Mor reached to his back pockets for his fairsabers. No, Luc would not come. Only Mor could save Dranian now. If Reval thought holding Dranian hostage would sway Luc, he did not know his own son.

A few more curses and threats were exchanged as Mor swept around the trunk of the tree. Shadows began striking Dranian's shoulders with their fairsaber hilts, and Dranian shook, his blinking turning rapid. Mor's chest tightened as he sensed the fairy's panic beginning to take over. He broke into a run—and skidded to a halt, swinging himself around another tree.

His eyes were wide, his faeborn heart hammering. He could have sworn he just saw…

Luc.

Mor peered around the tree. Shadow Fairies sniffed the air, looking around. He ducked in further to hide when they looked in his direction.

"It was more like the other way around, actually."

The Shadows moved out of the way, revealing a wild-eyed fairy with metallic-red hair and heart shaped lips, and bringing forth more memories than Mor wished to keep.

Luc began mouthing off to his father, and Mor thought he was dreaming. What was Luc doing here? Why did none of this make sense, and for the love of the sky deities, did Luc *want* to die? It was like being back in that clearing all over again when Reval Zelsor had stabbed his own son through the chest and Luc had risen from the dead while Mor watched from the thornbush. Only this time, Luc seemed ready for it. Like he knew it was coming and didn't care.

"I'm here now," Luc said, "so let the broken North Fairy be on his way before you awaken the wrath of his brothers."

His brothers. Mor came back to his senses and yanked out his phone. The phone rang a few times after he dialed. Cress still didn't answer, so Mor left a message.

"There's trouble. I'm at the park by…"

Mor choked as Reval sliced his palm and slapped his blood onto a lock binding Dranian's wrists.

"By…" Mor tried again, but his ear tilted to the Army and he went quiet, desperate to hear what was happening.

"If you want to stop me, perhaps you should stand in my way," Prince Reval said to Luc. It was an absurd suggestion. One that Mor thought Luc couldn't possibly even consider, except… Except that Luc shouldn't have come here at all. And he did.

Reval raised his fairsaber blade high over Dranian's neck, and Mor dropped his phone. He was three paces closer when Luc swept in and slashed Reval's blade aside. Mor blinked as Luc glanced back at Dranian and muttered something, then he turned back to Prince Reval.

"You were right about me. I planned to betray you once I was of age," he said, and Mor slapped a hand over his thundering chest. "We're less than a year away from our appointment on the mountain, aren't we? Fight me, Father," he said. "Let's see who's the more cunning fox."

"I have a better idea. How about some sport?" the Dark Prince countered.

"Stop deflecting. It makes me think you're afraid of me," Luc stated, crouching and preparing to charge his father—something Mor never thought he'd see in his faeborn lifetime.

But Reval ignored him. "What do the humans call it here again? A *goalie*? I'll try to kill him while he sits there. Block me, if you can. He takes the punishment for whatever you can't stop."

Mor's stomach dropped and he strode toward the Army after all, every apology he knew whispered in the wind, hoping this plea for forgiveness would find its way to Violet.

"How about a trade first?" Mor called, grabbing the attention of Prince Reval.

As soon as he said it, Mor knew the High Prince of the Dark Corner would recognize him as the village boy who had destroyed his reputation. From the corner of his eye, Mor saw Luc's head snap in his direction. He felt the fox's eyes burrowing into him. He felt Dranian looking at him, too. He felt the stares of the whole division he had attacked and abandoned piercing his fairy flesh where he stood.

But Mor tossed his fairsabers into the grass. "This is a game for Shadow Fairies," he said. Prince Reval's face flickered with recognition, then he glared. "Let's keep it between Shadows," Mor finished.

Luc looked like he'd been slapped. Then he looked furious, accusation on his twisting lips as he turned to face Mor, a question burning from his being in the manner of, *"What in the name of the sky deities are you doing here?"*

Of the two foxes, Luc's glare was perhaps worse.

Popping filled the air, and Mor was apprehended. He was torn into an airslip and appeared at Dranian's side. The backs of his legs were kicked, and he kneeled before the great foxes who ruled the armies of the Dark Corner of Ever. Luc did not take his glare off Mor.

"Mor…" Dranian rasped. The auburn-haired fairy looked dreadful. Mor wasn't sure if he could perform a rescue with Dranian in such condition, but he had to try. And he knew he couldn't do it alone.

"It's alright, Dranian, there's no need to panic. I'm here," Mor whispered. He finally met Luc's eyes as his arms were yanked forward and a metal bloodlock was forced onto his wrists. Luc showed no signs of understanding. His terrible gaze hadn't left Mor for a single second; his rosy lips had not moved from their frown.

Mor looked back at the Dark Prince who had once tried to steal his only good memories in hopes of creating eternal bad ones. "I've traded myself, now release him. He's injured." Mor nodded to Dranian, who shook his head in protest. "Let's deal with this like Shadows."

Prince Reval's lip curled. "I cannot believe my fox eyes," he said. "I deny your request for a trade, Trisencor. I deny your right to live, too."

An arrow spiralled from the Army, and Mor stiffened.

A black fairsaber sliced it in half a mere second before it would have impaled Mor's face. He swallowed, his eyes following the length of the black blade to Luc who held it. At Luc's wrist, Mor noticed a twist of branches with two white blossoms. He'd seen one of those before—when Prince Reval had given a disobedient fairy three days to live.

Luc finally stopped glaring at him. The fox took in a deep, long breath and let it out through his nose. He turned slowly to face Prince Reval, his jaw flexing with the motion.

"Game on," he said to his father.

Prince Reval sneered as he tied back his hair with a ribbon. "Since you now have an extra fairy, I shall have one, too." He waved a Shadow forward who raised a glistening pearl bow and a sheath of silver arrows likely coated in cold iron. Prince Reval placed his ruby on his tongue.

Mor watched Luc draw his own bead from his pocket. The young fox looked at it long and hard, not revealing a thing going through his cunning head. And then he ate it.

The Shadow bowman loaded a fresh arrow, aiming it for Mor's heart. Mor took in a breath and held it, relieved the Shadows weren't aiming for Dranian anymore. They'd be fools to target Dranian with a black-marked Shadow Fairy present.

Prince Reval raised his fairsabers, eyeing Luc as he plotted his first blow. "Obviously, you can't save yourself *and* them—" Reval's words lurched to a halt when the bowman released the arrow, and Luc...

Luc twisted around in front of Mor just in time to take it.

The metal arrow broke through the fox's back and came out his chest, stopping an inch from Mor's heart. Luc's face warped, his jaw setting, his lashes fluttering. "Are you ready, Trisencor?" he bit out.

Mor didn't know how to reply. He looked over at the bloodlock on Dranian's wrists. On his own wrists. Up at Luc again.

Luc spun, slashing with his left fairsaber and nearly catching Reval at the throat. The Prince tipped back to avoid the swing, and came up with one of his own. Luc's hand flashed out and grabbed the blade midair. Purple blood oozed between his fingers and sprinkled the grass—Reval's eyes widened.

Luc swung at Reval, forcing him back another step. The bowman quickly loaded another arrow as Luc dropped his grip on Reval's blade. The foxes exchanged a series of swings and misses too fast for most fairy eyes to behold. Luc marched after his father and raised his saber, but he didn't stab at Prince Reval—his blade went through the bowman.

The bowman gasped as Luc tore his blade back out, sending the quiver to the ground and a dozen cold iron arrows rolling through the grass.

"Take his place!" Reval barked at the Shadows. Two new war fae lifted bows and stepped into line, drawing arrows and taking aim.

Luc vanished. Shadow Fairies turned in all directions to give chase, looking up at the sky. But he reappeared facing Mor and Dranian as the bowmen released their arrows.

Arrows speared into him—one into his lower back, one through his shoulder. Luc buckled forward, barely catching himself on a knee. He slapped his hands together, smearing around his purple fairy blood. Mor blinked as the fox smacked his hands down on Mor's and Dranian's bloodlocks.

Luc cast Mor one last glare and rasped, "No need to thank me. We're enemies to the end, right?"

Mor wasn't sure if Luc was speaking to him or Dranian.

It didn't matter. The second the locks fell, Mor took the opportunity and grabbed Dranian, ripping him into the air. Dranian dripped blood, colours, and sweat into the gale. In the rush, Mor was vaguely aware of Luc below, shifting into the wind and grappling the ankles of any fairy who tried to follow them. Through the air threads, Mor escaped to the sight of Luc taking hit after hit. After hit.

After hit.

Three arrows impaled his body.

CHAPTER

22

Dranian Evelry and the Thing that Happened After

The insides of his eyelids were pink. Dranian peeled his eyes open, wondering for just a second why he'd been able to sleep in peace. He brought a hand to his forehead, realizing his head was thudding like a mountain village war drum. He winced and sat up, finding himself in pink bed sheets. He lifted a handful of the bedding to his face to study it. He knew these sheets.

This was Kate's bed, above Fae Café.

He lowered the sheets, his mind taking him back to his dream—the quiet one. The dream that wasn't really a dream at all, just an absence of anything.

Where had the girl gone? The dreamslipper? The girl with no name?

Why hadn't she shown up this time?

Dranian pulled the covers back and headed out of Kate's bedroom into the kitchenette. He slowed to a stop when he saw Mor was there. His faeborn heart tumbled when he realized Cress was there, too. And Lily. And Kate.

There was a tense silence in the room. Then Kate cleared her throat. "Are you okay—"

"Un-real, Dranian!" Lily said, and Kate scowled at her for interrupting.

Dranian opened his mouth to ask, but he closed it again, trying to determine what exactly he was in trouble for. He finally thought to ask Lily, "Did you tell them—?"

"I think the cat's out of the bag." Lily's folded arms tightened like it was taking all her human self-control not to reveal other things, too.

"What cat?" Cress asked. He began looking around. "I don't see a cat."

Mor closed his eyes in disbelief, and Dranian took the opportunity Cress provided by constantly misunderstanding human word expressions to come up with something proper to say. "It's not what it looks—"

"It's exactly what it looks like," Mor stated. "You were keeping company with that fox."

"Seriously, you guys keep cutting him off. Let him speak!" Kate snapped at Mor.

Mor folded his arms, mimicking Lily. The two looked like

poorly paid interrogation guards of the Silver Castle when they stood side by side like that.

Dranian's arm had felt heavy since the day it had stopped working properly. But right now, it felt as though his limb was filled with iron and weighing his whole body down.

"No more secrets!" Cress announced. "With Shayne on vacation, that makes me the next in charge, and I've had about enough of the not-telling-of-things. The next fairy—or human," he stole a sidelong glance at Kate and Lily, "who keeps a secret shall be forever banned from Fae Café and forced to work in the nearest amethyst salt mine for three months!"

"There aren't amethyst salt mines in the human realm," Dranian muttered, but no one heard him—no one apart from Lily. She must have, because she held Dranian's gaze, worry etched into her pretty human features. Worry about the one other secret the two of them were still keeping.

Dranian hadn't had a chance to tell her that he'd learned where Shayne was. That Shayne was in a mountain of trouble—that she may never see him again. The right thing to do would be to begin talking until everything was out in the open. But there was one matter Dranian could not shake, and that was the question of why Shayne had kept it a secret from everyone.

And for that, Dranian found he could not tell the others the truth about Shayne, because it was not his secret to tell. He cast Lily the tiniest shake of his head.

Her face fell, just a smidgen. She didn't let the others see though. She dropped her gaze to the floor and said nothing of Shayne or his mysterious whereabouts.

Also, Dranian learned in this exact moment that he hated keeping secrets. And he perhaps hated that he was too loyal to consider revealing them to others. He wished he was bad at it like Mor and Cress.

Mor sighed. "No one's getting banished from Fae Café," he objected. "But Cress is right. You should have asked us for help if Luc had you trapped in a roommate contract," he said to Dranian.

Dranian's lips thinned a little since that little detail wasn't one he'd shared with the group. This time, he glared over at Lily. She cleared her throat and looked off at the wall, suddenly seeming less tough.

"It's alright to ask for help, Dranian. Even Luc knew that," Mor said, mumbling the last part. Cress glanced at him in question, and Mor slammed his mouth shut.

"You're one to talk," Dranian muttered, wondering how everyone could forget that Mor had been the first brother to fly off and face Luc Zelsor on his own. "And the reason I didn't tell you wasn't because I was afraid of that fox. I kept it to myself because I was perfectly capable of handling it on my own!" Dranian stated, raising his voice a little. But as soon as the loud words came out, he wished he'd said them quietly.

Mor's jaw slid to the side. "Don't get snippy with me, you grump. That fox would kill us all if given the chance."

"Would he have? Because it looked to me like he was protecting you, Mor," Dranian snapped. "And me, for that matter."

Mor's mouth parted, his next response nonexistent. It was a look Dranian was sure everyone was used to seeing on *him*, and not on Mor. The others glanced between Mor and Dranian, and Dranian shifted his weight, realizing it was too late to take back his statement. His arm burned in anguish from his beating, and he felt like a fool before these perfectly whole fairies with great gifts and menacing reputations.

His shoulders dropped, reminding him of the physical agony that had found him because of Luc. Every little inch of movement sent pain shooting down his arms and into his body. "There is no one I am more loyal to than the fairies and humans in this room. But Luc Zelsor had every opportunity to leave me to die, to run to a faraway place, and to never return to face his fate. And he came back instead. Because of that, I'm now here with you all."

"What are you trying to say, exactly?" Cress asked. His eyes felt a little colder than normal. "Are you proposing we get involved in that father-son fox fight? That is preposterous, Dranian! Don't you know the cost if we show up anywhere near them?! Shayne's bargain will become void, and they'll come for us!"

Dranian looked at the floor. He wasn't sure what he was asking. If there was even a question to be asked. "They stole me from my bed. They attacked us first," he said.

Mor travelled to the window and gazed down at the street. "They will take Luc, they will leave, and this will be over. One

238

thing I will never do again is put our humans in danger," he said. "I won't risk Violet again. I won't join a war if she's the cost." Even though he said the words, his face told a different story. There was a crease between his brows that Dranian had only ever seen when Mor was either lying or was holding back what he really wanted to say. Dranian had seen that very look on Mor when Luc had taken the first arrow through the chest.

Cress tugged Kate closer to his side. She cast Cress a small smile of assurance, but Lily had an entirely different reaction. She looked bothered by Mor's statement. Dranian eyed her rigid stance. It was almost as if the female was offended for being considered too weak and breakable to defend herself, should the wars come. But she kept her thoughts to herself. "I have to go to work," she said, pulling her bag off the counter. Something fell out, and Dranian hopped over to pick it up, suddenly feeling the need to be of service to everyone more than ever.

He held up a plastic rectangle with Lily's photo on it, dangling from a cloth necklace. Dranian recognized it as the mystical item she'd used to gain access at Desmount Tech Industries.

A fast blush hit Lily's face as she grabbed it and stuffed it in her bag, glancing around to see if anyone had noticed it. "Thanks," she muttered. Dranian watched her head out the door and listened to her footsteps down the stairs.

Behind him, there were two fairies with humans to protect. Cress wanted nothing to do with the Shadow Army. Mor *pretended* he wanted nothing to do with the Shadow Army. Either way, his brothers were right; meddling with the fox fight was a bad idea. And Dranian had always put his loyalty first and obeyed whatever orders Cress came up with. Today would be no exception—*no one* wanted to get their hands dirty with fox blood. What was a fairy like Dranian to do anyway with one arm and no Shayne to jump aboard his reckless idea?

But then there was Lily, and that special little *thing* Lily had.

It was an outrageously irrational solution. Not Dranian's style, but perhaps a way to keep everyone happy, and alive.

Except Cress. Cress wouldn't be happy. He might make Dranian eat rocks.

Even so, Dranian was sure his own typical way of doing things wouldn't get the job done this time. For the first moment in his faeborn life, Dranian asked himself the question, *"What if I did whatever Shayne would do in this situation?"* Shayne was utterly reckless. However, he was also very effective.

"I'll be back," Dranian lied. He headed for the stairs and swept down with silence and grace, the complete opposite to the stomping parade Lily had performed. The café was closed, the fireplace unlit. Dranian realized he missed the place a little. Going down to part time had taken something from him, and he swore that if he survived the next twenty-four hours, he would return to work full time.

He caught up to Lily just outside. "Wait, Human." Then he thought better of the address, and corrected with, "Lily."

When Lily turned around, Dranian paused, realizing he didn't have anything planned. He looked off and fiddled with a loose thread on the hem of his bloody shirt. She shot him an odd look. And so, Dranian did what he thought Shayne might do. He opened his arms wide, and with a perfectly straight face, he walked at Lily.

She looked at him like he was crazy, even taking a step back, but he caught her first and wrapped his arms around her to fasten her into a hug. "Have a good day at work," he said in his monotone voice.

When he let her go, Lily's face appeared a blend of wondering if he'd lost his mind, and looking like she might slap him.

It was dreadfully difficult, but... Dranian stretched his face, pulling with all his might. He created a slow smile, as wide as it could go.

Finally, Lily put her hands on her hips. "Did you eat mush-rooms you found in the grass?" she asked. "Or are you actually out of your mind?"

Dranian's lopsided smile fell. "Never mind." He turned and strutted away, choosing not to go back into the café. He headed toward the bus stop instead, listening to Lily's sigh of disbelief behind him as she went on her way.

Dranian stole a quick look back. As soon as Lily was around the corner, he pulled the plastic rectangle with Lily's picture from his pocket. He flicked the cloth necklace with a satisfied nod, and he winced as he tried to ignore the shooting pains in his left arm from even the smallest movement.

Desmount Tech Industries was a wild jungle of crystal banners, secret entrances, and watching eyes. Dranian kept a straight, unsuspicious face as he battled the glass panels for access to the forbidden building. He brushed the dust off himself as he came into the lobby and drew out Lily's magic picture. A few humans glanced up at him, but no one raised their voices or asked questions. He slapped the picture down on a clear box thingy as he had seen Lily do, and a bar moved out of the way so he could pass.

Dranian conquered the staircase with minimal huffing and pain. He rounded into the hall and found the room Lily had taken him to before. When he was sure no souls were around, he slipped in and closed the door behind him.

There he gazed upon the fire-breathing, dragon-like mechanism hanging high upon the wall.

Saving Luc Zeslor wasn't going to be easy. But Dranian would do it, and he would do it on his own, because he was capable. Because even though Dranian was the one with the broken arm, Luc had considered Dranian to be far less broken than him. And it wasn't until Dranian had witnessed the fox come face to face with his devils that Dranian knew that to be true.

But it wasn't just for Luc. Dranian was doing this for Mor, too. Because, though no one else could see it, it was so utterly obvious that Mor cared about Luc, the way Mor always cared about everyone.

Also, Dranian was doing it for Shayne. The others—and Luc—would find that out soon enough.

And last, Dranian was doing it for Cress. Because with Cress and Mor having precious humans to protect, Dranian would not, and could not, ask them to return to the Ever Corners and wage war upon the House of Lyro. But maybe, *just maybe*, Luc could do it—if he stayed alive.

How absurd this plan felt.

Dranian was going to do it anyway.

CHAPTER

23

Luc Zelsor and His Last Breath

Being dragged back to the Dark Corner by his ankles would have been better than this. The Shadow Army beat Luc senseless in the air first, hidden away from the sight of humans who hadn't a clue that fairies were passing by overhead, brushing their faces as a wisp of wind, tugging at their clothes in a gale, or slipping through their hair as nothing more than a breeze.

Reval went in and out of Luc's vision. He was a monster in the sky, his hair fluttering, his eyes bright, his black sabers drawn. He hovered, always just a gust away, watching everything. There was only blackness in the Dark Prince's bones—Luc had always known it. Now he got to see it firsthand. In fact, it would be the last thing he ever saw.

When Luc's chest was so full of holes that the wind nearly sailed through him, the Shadows dropped him. He spiralled, being sucked down toward the realm's floor with not a seed of energy left to catch himself. His hands numbly searched the air for purchase, never finding grip, never finding a promise.

As he fell past a spoked roof and into the shadow of a tall building, his fox bead slid over his tongue, reminding him what he was. That where other fairies often failed and died, he had an extra push that had saved him before. He wasn't sure if he could find it, if it was still there after everything in his chest had been ripped out. But he closed his eyes and dug deep into himself, into his gift of the sky deities, into his iron-coated will.

It wasn't much, but he found one last sparkle of vigor. With it, he slipped out of his fall, catching himself on a passing wind.

It was a gong show of a catch. Luc tore off his path and dropped himself again, shooting his precious body sideways and plummeting through a glass window. A chyme-like music filled his ears as glass shattered and shards sprinkled over a long, empty room.

He was dead as soon as he hit the floor.

His rhythms had relocated into his head, loud and deep.

Luc squinted as the pounding filled his ears and overcame his senses. He could smell and taste the sound; it carried the fragrance of blood and the salty flavour of sweat. Tugging sensations birthed over his flesh and deep into his body as his wounds began to close themselves up.

Something at his neck quivered, and Luc's hand soared to his chest. His eyes flew open, and he sat up. He raised his foxtail necklace and watched the glossy threads of his second-last tail evaporate and return to the sky deities.

One left.

Just one spare.

Two more deadly strikes and he would not come back. Then he would be just another fox legend young fairies might read about in old books, and if he was lucky, they might whisper about him before bedtime.

A pale-skinned hand appeared and tugged the necklace from him. Luc almost snatched it back, almost panicked. Reval was crouched down, examining the one thing standing between him having a son and no longer having one.

Would he really do it? Luc no longer knew if his father wanted to keep him alive. Luc was, and perhaps always had been, just another threat to the High Prince. Something that stood in his way, just like Luc's mother had.

Luc did not want to think about his mother, but he could not stop himself now. As he stared into the glimmering, wicked eyes of the male who had sent her away, then kidnapped her, and was likely starving her to death—Luc's energy came back tenfold. He reached for his last spare life, tore it from Reval's grip, and tucked it back beneath his shirt where it belonged.

Behind the Dark Prince was an enormous lobby with tall, cathedral-like ceilings. Long tables were stationed neatly around the room, apart from the one Luc had smashed when he flew in. Books filled shelves at the far end, and button-covered computers lined the walls on separate desks. It appeared to be some sort of human academy or study space.

"You started with nine, and you were down to five when we caught you. How shameful." Reval's voice was cold and detached, and Luc knew now that his suspicion was correct. Reval had already separated himself from his fox child. Reval was going to kill him.

"How many do *you* have left?" Luc challenged, and he rose from the floor, scanning the room for his fairsabers. But, naturally, his fairsabers were gone. It was the first thing the Shadows had wrestled out of his hands. Reval had stabbed him through the heart after that. It was the first life Luc had lost of the five that he had worked so hard to save. It had been a quick death show after that as he'd been impaled over and over.

At Luc's question, Reval stood, his appearance growing colder. "Oh dear," Luc rasped, cocking his head. "Is that a difficult question to answer?" He glanced down at Reval's collar where a gold chain was tucked safely below his breastplate. "Why, Father?" Luc asked, studying the subtle tightness of the fool's throat, his face, his shoulders. A true study of a fairy if there ever was one.

Luc found his wickedly broad smile. It had been a bit since

he'd used his smile. He'd missed the feeling, even if it did put a sting in his cracked lips.

"Could it be that your father stole all your fox lives on that shadowy mountain twenty-five years ago?" Luc asked. The sky darkened outside; an icy breeze skittered past the windows of the building. The floor seemed to shake below Luc's legs, the desks all rattling a little. Luc huffed in disbelief. "My dear mother told me that story. And now that I'm thinking about it, a female that clever couldn't have been captured by the likes of you. She's not really starving in a pit somewhere, is she? Be honest." Luc watched his father's face very carefully—more carefully than he ever had.

The Dark Prince drew his right fairsaber, ending the conversation, and Luc knew it was all over now. So, he decided to go out with a laugh.

It started as just a chuckle, but the more he thought about it, the more real his cackling became. All this time… if he had simply struck first, perhaps he might have spared himself, and his mother, and the Dark Corner, all this dread. And now Reval would rule the Dark Corner as the hollow-chested male who had destroyed every fairy who had ever been close to him. He was a monster; a poison to the fair folk. He would turn the Dark Corner to ash and let the villages starve to death. He would probably assassinate the Dark Queene with his bloodthirsty Army. Luc had seen it coming, yet he had not moved quickly enough. If by some miracle the sky deities would give him more lives to spare, Luc would not make the same mistake twice.

Reval's blade plunged into his chest, and Luc gasped. Torrents of wind raked through his hair, reaching into his soul and ripping out the last spare life he'd been gifted at birth. He fell back, meeting the blackness once again.

There was shouting somewhere deep in the folds of space around him. It sounded as nothing more than a watery echo. Luc didn't want to wake. He didn't want to open his eyes, lest his last life be taken. But perhaps it was time. Perhaps he had fought long enough. Perhaps this was his destiny after all, to be cursed as a nine tailed fox. Given nine extra lives. Nine chances that ultimately were his ruin and the very cause of his death in the end, like so many of the legendary foxes before him.

But when he peeled his tired eyes open, he saw the brightest orange he'd ever gazed upon. Melted gold, tearing across the air, blanketing everything in sight. He didn't recognize what it was at first, but then he knew. He knew it was a sign. A miracle; perhaps the one he had been waiting for. The sky deities' answer to the call of a dying fox.

He dragged his gaze slowly to the Dark Prince standing above him. Reval turned in circles, shouting orders that got lost and muffled in Luc's ears. Luc could not quite see clearly; he couldn't hear most things yet, either. It was too soon, but he did not waste his one chance. The golden gift from the sky.

Luc rose, rolling to his feet in one swift motion. He ripped the fairsaber from Reval's hand, and he plunged it into the Dark Prince's chest. Right into the place where a heart was supposed to be, if a fairy like him were capable of possessing one.

Roaring thunder from outside became sharper in Luc's ears as he stared at Reval's gasping face.

The rest of the room slithered into Luc's consciousness—the shouting Shadow Fairies, the assembling Army, all the pointing at some fire-wielding creature leaping from desk to desk in the corner of Luc's vision. But he kept his gaze on Reval Zelsor. A male who was not, by any means, his father. Nor had he ever been a single day in his life.

When Luc tore the blade back out, he grabbed the gold chain at Reval's throat and held onto it as the Prince fell. The chain snapped and slid from its hiding place, detaching from its owner, raised in Luc's hand. Luc looked at it for a long time, even after Reval's body went still on the floor.

On the end of the Dark Prince's chain were no tails. The gold clasp meant to hold many lives, empty.

Luc lowered the chain to his side, staring out at nothing. All this time, his father was just one fight away from death, from Luc being free forever. All this time, the Prince's arrogance was a mask for his fear. He let everyone believe he was invincible with nine lives to spare.

Yet, he was no different from any other single-life fairy whose blood ran purple.

It became the poetry Luc got lost in for the next few moments. Then, he became aware that he stood in the very centre of chaos. He felt warm. *Burning*, in fact.

He looked around to find the ceiling on fire, the windows scorched black, desks strewn and smashed... Shadow Fairies were either dead, falling to the floor trying desperately to breathe, or fleeing into the air.

Luc coughed as smoke filled his lungs.

His lungs... His precious, last set of lungs.

He slammed his arm over his mouth to shield himself from the toxic fumes, and he spun, trying to gather what was happening, why everything was on fire, and...

Luc dropped his arm when he beheld a fairy with messy auburn hair marching over the desktops with a satchel on his back, breathing fire from a large black snout like an ancient beast. The three-legged guard dog blasted Shadow Fairies with little mercy, rendering them too weak to airslip and filling the room with the most repulsive-smelling fumes of melting fae flesh Luc had ever inhaled.

Luc coughed again, then he trotted over and hopped onto the desk.

Dranian nearly blasted him with fire, but Luc raised his hands quickly. "Oh dear... Can we call a truce?" he asked.

Dranian lowered the fire beast's snout, and—to Luc's true wonder—the side of the fool's mouth tugged up, just a smidgen.

Enough that it might have been considered by some to be a smile. It was a strange, pleasant moment until Luc grabbed him by the shoulder and hurtled him off the desk.

Dranian tumbled to the floor with his fire beast as Luc stabbed his father's fairsaber into a Shadow Fairy in the wind. The fool's blade was swinging precisely where Dranian had been standing. The fairy buckled into a heap, and Luc kicked him off the desk. He hopped down to Dranian's side.

"What do you say, North Fairy? Should we slip out of here, or should we take them all down so they don't come back again?" he asked, facing away from Dranian and moving into a defensive stance as the Shadows who were left raced in to close the gap.

"Do you feel up to it?" Dranian's words were almost too quiet to hear.

"No. I'm hot and I *feel like* eating ice cream. But we don't always get ice cream when we want it, do we?" Luc reassessed his blade then crouched to steal one off a Shadow body on the floor. He twisted both in his grip, getting a feel for them.

"Let's fight," Dranian decided. He raised the fire beast and hit a button. A wave of orange-gold splashed through the room, beautifully devouring everything in its path and leaving a trail of black ash.

Luc struck the first Shadow Fairy, locking blades then twisting to strike at another at the same time. He took them both down just as the roaring of the fire beast ceased. He spun back to Dranian.

The fool's green eyes went round. Dranian shook the beast a

little, then hit the button again. Nothing happened. "Queensbane," he cursed, ripping the satchel off and drawing his spear instead.

"Is this a joke?" Luc complained. He slashed a Shadow Fairy's arm who came too close. "Did you feed it before you came?"

"I didn't know it would run out of faeborn fire!" Dranian said, hurtling his spear into a fairy. Then he whirled to Luc. "Let's not fight," he said, changing his mind. "Let's do the running away thing."

Luc kicked back a Shadow and rubbed his temples as he followed Dranian. The North Fairy leapt over bleeding fairies to fetch his spear. "Fine. I'll hunt them down later or something," Luc sighed. He grabbed Dranian's shoulder when a loud, booming crack sounded through the building, and Luc spun.

A familiar young human female marched in through the wide double doors at the end of the room. She held a gun, and she fired it at anything Shadowy that moved. Twenty humans in uniforms trailed in behind her. Their weapons were unusual and strangely accurate, bullets bending around corners and swerving in arcs. Luc thought of his last life and had the overwhelming urge to escape. But Dranian appeared at his side, seeming less worried as the police officers waged war upon the Shadow Army division.

Though humans were a far lesser species to fairies, Luc had to admit, he was slightly impressed. There wasn't a single tremor of fear in Lily Baker's rhythms. She aimed. She fired. She destroyed.

"Lily Baker," Luc mused, studying the ink paintings over her outstretched arms beyond her rolled-up sleeves. When she turned,

Luc spotted a sewn inscription across her back that read: TRUE NORTH STRONG. The other officers wore the badge, too. "Is that truly her real name?" Luc asked Dranian curiously. Dranian seemed to choose not to answer.

Shadow Fairies lost their balance one after another, and Dranian nudged Luc toward the side of the room. "Their shots will find you, too," he warned, and Luc's mouth twisted into a scowl. He'd wanted to watch the show. But he reluctantly reached for Dranian's shoulder.

They vanished to the sound of thunderous cracks and a falling Shadow Army division.

24

Dranian Evelry: Master of Secrets and Lies
and Other Treacherous Things

Two fairies smelling of smoke collapsed onto an apartment floor. A dog with a flappy, loose tongue came racing to them, licking faces and barking. Dranian patted Dog-Shayne on the head, but Luc made a repulsed noise beside him.

"Why must everything be so wet?" he asked, wiping off his drool-covered cheek with his sleeve.

"Let's get cleaned up." Dranian winced as he inched his way up to stand. He was far more sore than he cared to admit. The pains in his shoulder and arm had become nearly unbearable. By the time he got to his feet, he realized Luc was already standing, waiting.

Luc blinked. Then he poked Dranian's shoulder, and it was so dreadful, Dranian nearly buckled and fell to the floor again.

Luc sighed. "I'd ask what you were thinking going up against Shadows in your condition, but I suppose I don't really care what you were thinking since the result is me being alive," he said.

Dranian rubbed his shoulder. "It's because of you I have these bruises," he reminded him.

Luc shrugged. "Maybe. Maybe you should have been more careful. What were you doing when the Army snuck up on you in the first place? How did they manage to get close enough to kidnap you without you sniffing them?"

Dranian thought about his dream—the one he'd been deeply lost in when the Shadows came. "Never mind that," he mumbled. "Get cleaned up so we can be off to Fae Café before sundown." He headed toward his room to find fresh clothes, all the while thinking about the moment Lily had come marching into the smoky turmoil, gun raised, and had abolished a pack of Shadow Fairies with her own army.

And how he'd completely stolen her fire-breathing thing.

He was in for an arse-whooping from just about everyone now.

Something blocked the light of his doorway after he came in. He turned to find Luc standing there with his arms folded.

"What in the name of the sky deities would make you think I would go to Fae Café, of all places? Hmm?" A large scowl took up most of his face.

"Because Mor wants to know if you're alive," Dranian said,

and Luc's face changed. "And because the next part of my plan involves you."

Dranian's room filled the with the sound of Luc's snort-laugh. "You made plans for *me*? I think I'm finished with letting others make plans and expecting me to fulfil them. I might as well have stayed in the Army if I wanted to do that."

"I saved you," Dranian said, "so come to Fae Café this one time. For Mor."

He turned to face Luc, waiting for his decision.

Luc glared a little. The fox slid his jaw back and forth. He looked off.

Dranian tuned Luc out after several minutes. Luc grumbled the whole way through the apartment, the whole way down the hall and descending the stairs, the whole way down the sidewalk, and for the whole bus ride. He never offered to airslip them to the café so they'd get there faster. He even made Dranian pay his bus fee.

Finally, halfway through the bus ride, Dranian said, "Closure is important when it comes to things that are broken."

Luc's grumbling went quiet. The fox's glare drilled into the side of Dranian's head. "Are you trying to therapist me?" he asked in disbelief. "I cannot be therapist-ed. I study others and therapist them when necessary. Or sometimes I kill them if it becomes too annoying, but either way, everyone I cross ends up resting in peace one way or another."

"Except Mor," Dranian mumbled. Then, a little brighter, he said, "It doesn't matter anyway. Letting Mor know you're alive is only half the reason we're going. I'm sure by now Lily has called the others and told them of my mischief—"

Luc raised a brow. "Mischief? That's not the word I would use."

"—and so, I'm to deal with that first, and my plan second."

Luc rolled his eyes and rested his face against his fist. "These seats are far too close together. I can hardly breathe."

The bus slowed to a stop and the two fairies exited. Dranian led the way down the block, tugging his jacket tighter as the chilly wind swept down the street, picking up dry leaves and tossing them about. He followed the scent of fresh baking and lattes to Fae Café's front door.

"You might like the coffee here." Even though Dranian spoke with little enthusiasm, he meant it. "It's—"

"Oh, stop. I'm going to hate it." Luc yanked his own coat tighter and folded his arms as Dranian opened the door.

When he came in, Dranian took inventory of the dozen or so human customers milling about or seated at tables and engaged in quiet chatter. Cress came out of the kitchen in a burgundy apron and stopped just outside the kitchen's new swinging doors.

Dranian loosened his collar and swallowed, sure he could taste phantom rocks on his tongue. But he cleared his throat and went to meet his former Prince. While keeping eye contact, Cress drew his phone out of his pocket and hit a button with his thumb. He lifted it to his ear slowly as Dranian approached, and he mumbled something into it.

Mor suddenly appeared behind the counter with a *pop*, and a few humans shrieked from their tables. Mor looked past Dranian. He kept his gaze on Luc for a moment, not revealing anything, and then brought his attention back to Dranian again. There wasn't necessarily relief on his face, but his shoulders relaxed a little.

Suddenly, Mor smiled. Not in a kind, *"It's alright, we forgive you,"* way, but in a way like he felt the need to laugh and was doing everything in his faeborn power to *not* laugh. "Did you really fight my old Shadow Army division with one arm?" he asked, and Cress growled.

"Don't make this funny, Mor!" he shouted. "I said no more secrets! And I said we weren't going to get involved in the fox fight! And I said… all kinds of other important things that I can't remember at the moment!"

Mor smothered away his grin. "I'm sorry," he mumbled to Cress. "I just can't stop picturing it."

"You could have been slaughtered, you faeborn-cursed fool!" Cress roared at Dranian. He marched across the last of the open space and put his finger in Dranian's face. "You are lucky there are no amethyst salt mines in the human realm!" His cold glare cut over to Luc. "And what is that wretched fox doing here? He's filling my café with the horrid stench of Shadow Fairies!"

Mor's face fell. "Careful," he said, "I'm a Shadow, too."

Cress had sniffed with ample drama. "Nope. It's not you, Mor." He glared at Luc again.

"I don't smell like Shadow Fairies." Luc finally entered the conversation. Dranian glanced back to find him leaning against a table where two young, female humans blinked up at him. "My fragrance is sweet and alluring, in case you haven't noticed." He glanced down at one of the females. "Isn't that right?" he asked her, pulling his heart-shaped lips into a handsome smile.

One female blushed; the other giggled.

Cress made a face that looked as though he might barf on the café floor.

"You're right Mor, I've had a busy day," Dranian said, turning back. "And that's why I've decided to go on a vacation. I'll be leaving soon, and I'll... send you a human post card." He looked over at the cookie painting on the wall so that Mor would not see that he was lying through his teeth.

"You still haven't explained why there's a fox in my café," Cress said, "or why you charged into a fox fight in the first place and started burning everything alive."

Dranian let out a long breath. It was time to come clean—about one thing, at least. "Well, Luc Zelsor and I have become dog-owning allies. F...F..." Why could he not spit out the word? "*FRIENDS*, even..." It was a strange shout, and he wondered if he was making the situation worse. But Luc lifted from the table and sauntered to his side.

"The *best* of friends, actually," he said, reaching for a basket of cookies on the counter. Dranian looked over at the fox in surprise. Luc's dark gaze flickered up to Mor as he took a cookie. The two locked their brown and silver eyes. "Does that bother you, Mor?" Luc asked. He took a bite of cookie and waited.

Dranian dragged a hand down the side of his face and butted in. "Anyway, now that you know I'm going on a *vacation*," he articulated, "you don't have to worry about me or wonder if I've gone missing."

Luc dragged his gaze over, casting Dranian a doubtful look that made it clear he wasn't fooling anyone with his stuttering lie.

Dranian cleared his throat. "I'll be going to pack now," he stated. He turned and exhaled the breath he was holding as soon as his back was to everyone. Then he headed out, relieved that apart from Shayne's one secret, he no longer had to keep any more secrets, whatsoever.

His phone buzzed in his pocket, and he drew it out as he headed to the door. It was a word message from Lily:

Dranian, don't tell anyone about my team showing up to face off with those fairies. The others don't know about my fairy-hunting taskforce. Please, keep this a secret. I only told the others that I happened to witness the fight, not that I was a part of it.
Please, please, please, PLEASE.

The message ended with a teensy-tiny yellow smiley face containing large, innocent eyes. Dranian pursed his lips, his grip tightening on his phone and a low growl rumbling in his throat.

Not. Again.

He realized Luc was beside him when the fox sighed. "You café fools are all the same," he said with his snoopy eyes on the message. "I've lost track of all the things you don't tell each other." But he couldn't seem to stop the broad smile from taking over his face. "It's hilarious."

Dranian shoved his phone away. "I paid for your bus ride last time. So, you can pay for mine this time," he grumbled.

"If I must." Luc grabbed his arm, and Dranian was lurched forward.

His surroundings disappeared and reappeared as a quaint apartment, his feet hitting the floor with a thud. He put a hand on his stomach so he wouldn't be sick at the unexpectedness of it. Dog-Shayne padded over and sat at his feet, panting.

"Why did you have to push Mor's buttons?" Dranian muttered at Luc.

Luc headed to the door and kicked off his shoes. "This might come as a surprise, but I've been pushing Mor's buttons since the day I met him. He would think something was suspicious if I suddenly stopped." He stretched and yawned like he was ready for a nap.

Dranian folded his arms and tapped a finger in thought. "What happens if the Shadow Army division doesn't return to the Dark

Corner? Will the Dark Queene send hunters to find them? Will the human realm be flooded with spies?"

Luc lifted his arm into a shrug. "I'm not sure what my diabolical grandmother will do," he said, "but it doesn't matter to me. I won't be here."

Dranian unfolded his arms, dropping them. "You're leaving?" He hadn't even told Luc his plan yet.

"I have something to do in the Ever Corners. It's..." Luc's lips twisted in annoyance. "...a long story."

"Wait... *I'm* going to the Ever Corners," Dranian stated. "I was hoping to drag you along as payment for saving your life."

Luc grunted. "We're even now, North Fairy. I saved your life, you saved mine. I owe you nothing." He bristled. "And I don't have time to help you on whatever little scheme you're plotting. My problem is bigger, I guarantee it. If I don't hurry, someone will starve to death." His gaze dropped and he nudged the edge of the living space rug with his toe. "In fact, she probably already has. I'm likely walking into a trap."

Dranian considered that and sighed. "I suppose you can't come with me to save Shayne, then."

Luc blinked. Then he burst out laughing. "That fool who shot me through the heart? I'd rather die."

There was a loud knock on the door. Luc hopped over to open it, but he didn't open it wide enough for Dranian to see who was on the other side. Luc smiled, seeming to debate whether he was going to let the person past him.

The door was kicked open when he didn't offer an invitation, and Lily walked in. She still wore her uniform, she still smelled of smoke. Her light hair was tousled and falling out at all sides, her blue eyes blazing like an angry crossbeast.

"You want to know how I found you, Dranian?" she asked before he had a chance to greet her. "My *flame shooter* went missing." Her tone gave off a different feeling than the cute smiley face in her word message had. "Did you seriously think I was dumb enough to make weapons like that without putting trackers in them?" she asked.

Dranian realized she wanted him to answer that question. But the problem was that he didn't know what a tracker was, or what she was even talking about really. "No?" he guessed.

"Unreal! I can't believe you stole my weapon, went to face off with a bunch of thug fairies, and just burned the life out of a historic building!" she stressed. "I don't have a way to explain all that to the press! I finally got my department to take this fairy stuff seriously and partner with Desmount Tech, and now the whole project might get shut down because of what you did."

From the corner of his eye, Dranian saw Luc lean against the wall to watch them, as though Lily and Dranian were in an episode of one of the late-night thriller shows he'd become obsessed with.

"I did it for Shayne," Dranian said.

Lily opened her mouth to accuse him of more, but her tone seemed to change. "What?" she said instead.

"Human," he said, then corrected himself with, "*Lily*." Dranian spoke more sternly now. "You asked me to keep a secret for you, which I've now discovered I loathe doing. So, you will keep one for me as well." He swallowed, his mind returning him back to that dream, back to that girl—no, a fully grown female now—and what she had told him. "I know where Shayne is," he said.

Lily's brows tilted in, her height seeming to deflate. "Where?" she asked. "Where's Shayne?" Her voice cracked on his name.

Dranian felt an unexpected flit of panic that had no business showing up. His hands found a tremor, but he wasn't shaken enough to lose control. Not now. Not standing before Lily. Not with what he had to do.

"Shayne is in the Ever Corners," he stated. "He went back to his birth home." From the wall, Luc watched curiously, studying Lily the most. "You see, his brother must kill him to gain the highest chair of the Lyro family," he finished.

Lily looked back and forth between Dranian's eyes, a shield of caution sliding over her expression. She masked her stance, her tone, even her voice when she asked, "What does that mean?"

"It means he'll die there." Dranian despised the words on his own tongue. He despised the thought in his heart, the worry that he may not get there in time. That it may already be too late.

A beat of silence filled the room until Luc lifted from the wall and murmured, "Hmm." Both Dranian and Lily frowned at him, and Luc lifted his hands in feign apology. "Her rhythms just went wild, didn't you notice?" he said to Dranian. And then, when Dranian didn't reply, Luc shrugged and walked off to the kitchen so he didn't have to be involved. On his way, he mumbled, "It's telling."

"I don't understand. Why would he go to that place if it means he'll die?" Lily's question came out coarse. "Why wouldn't he even let me know, or... Why wouldn't he even say goodbye?"

Dranian didn't know how to answer that. But Lily wouldn't take silence as a reply; she grabbed a fistful of his sleeve. Her eyes glossed over.

"Shayne can't just go die!" she said.

Dranian carefully peeled her fingers off his shirt to free himself. "On that, we agree," he said. He glanced toward the kitchen. Luc had disappeared into his room. "Which is why I'm leaving at dawn. But I didn't go through all that suffering on my own today just to drag Mor and Cress into this. So, if I get worried you're going to tell them, Lily Baker, I will enslave you and make you mute."

He wasn't sure he had ever threatened a female. Part of him liked the feeling of it, the other part was worried Lily would draw her fairy-slaying weapon and end him. He cringed as her mind seemed to work, as she stared at him long and hard without blinking.

Forever seemed to pass before she spoke again. "What exactly are the odds of me dying if I set foot in the Ever Corners?" she asked.

Dranian felt a mix of feelings sink into his faeborn heart. The greatest of them was worry for this human, that she didn't realize the gravity of what she was asking.

Then, from his bedroom, Luc yelled through the door, "You won't die, dear Lily. You'll be captured and sold to nobles. Then you'll be fed all sorts of enchanted foods, forced to dance until your feet bleed, and dressed up in gaudy gowns... possibly pitted into a fight against a creature twice your size at a banquet arena." Luc swung the door open so Dranian and Lily could hear him clearly. "You won't die. But you'll wish you were dead."

Lily went a shade paler. Her slender throat constricted, but she stood tall. "I don't care what happens to me. It would be good to go for research. I'll wear a bodycam, and I'll... take notes," she said in what felt like an attempt to convince herself. Dranian meant to protest, to try and make her realize just how dreadful it could be for a human among so many manipulative fairies, but Lily lifted her chin, looked him dead in the eyes, and said, "I have to go pack. Don't you dare leave without me, Dranian."

Dranian's chest filled with dread. He looked past Lily to Luc for help, but Luc was smiling, widely. Wickedly. "Oh dear. I had a plan, you know. But I think I've just been overcome with desire to see you in that terrible situation," he said to Lily.

Lily bit her lips together. She cast the fox a daggered look as she turned and headed for the door, her hand idly finding its way to the weapon at her hip. "Maniac," she muttered.

Luc chuckled, his mouth twisting into a satisfied smile.

The apartment door slammed when Lily left. At the same time, Luc closed his bedroom door again.

Dranian was left alone, standing in the middle of the living space, wide-eyed and stunned.

A second later, Luc poked his head back out of his bedroom and said, "Should we go get groceries for our trip?"

The Faeborn End of One Thing

&

The Faeborn Beginning of Another

Thank you for reading *Wanted: A Roommate Who Isn't Evil*!

If you liked this book, please consider leaving a review. Each and every review means the world to me!

Not finished with the assassins? Do you want to find out what happens to Shayne?

Join Jennifer Kropf's newsletter at www.JenniferKropf.com to be alerted of the release of *Fake Dating a Human 101*, Book 4 in the *High Court of the Coffee Bean* series.

Bonus Fun:
Join the **Fae Café contest**
Post a book photo/video/quote/your favorite moment of the High Court of the Coffee Bean books to Tiktok or Instagram and use the hashtag #faecafecontest in your post.

Every season, a winner will be chosen, and a special fairy present will be mailed to someone's door!
(open internationally)

Want more books?

Read the Winter Souls series by Jennifer Kropf, a Christmas-themed Christian Fantasy series for ages 10+, loved by teens and adults alike:

A SOUL AS COLD AS FROST

A HEART AS RED AS PAINT

A CROWN AS SHARP AS PINES

A BEAST AS DARK AS NIGHT

CAROLS AND SPIES

ACKNOWLEDGEMENTS

First, thank you to God who made me weird enough to write fantasy books. I'm overwhelmed by the opportunities I've been given in my life because of a little faith.

Next, thank you to my editor, Melissa Cole, for laughing with me through all the nonsense (not only in this book, but also in life.) I love being a part of team #melissacoleedits.

Thank you to my agent, Brent Taylor, for bringing me aboard the Triada US team and putting this book series into the hands of so many amazing readers across the world. I never imagined the High Court of the Coffee Bean series could be read in so many languages and reach so far across this planet.

Thank you to my Patrons: Sarah Breed, Roy & Sarah, Audrey Moore, austengirl_710, Betsy Squires, Anne Lawson, Eden, Stephanie York, Vickie Grider, Amy Ovall, Bella, Lydia Woodward, Mae, Amanda Shafer, Danielle, Redlac, Lyndsey Hall, Kanyon Kiernan, Emma

Walker, Candy S, Kari Grindel, Jennifer Negrete, Sunny L Pullen, Cass, Hai Simis, Sajra Tobak, Gabby Lucas, Mae.reads, Gaming with Elfey, Jess, Ira Glu, Austengirl, ThiccTeacup, Nebula, Judy Rogers, Amber Gamble, Erin Pearce, Fiona, Cheryl Sims, Yajaiara Aguilar, Jodi, Anastassia Vales, Courtney, Laman Samo, Mimi Anderson, and Kendra. This group has become my safe place to strategize, and you guys are the dream team.

Thank you to Astrid Johnsson for being a true master of storytelling. Your advice is worth a chest of gold. You always help take my books to the next level. You are remarkable.

Thank you to my street team (the Book Nerd Herd), and to every single one of my ARC readers. Your reviews and enthusiasm are like a magical energy drink that keeps me going.

And, once again, a big thank you needs to go to the hilarious side of BookTok who offered ideas and so much joy for this book series when I first pitched the idea of fae living among humans and having to navigate through everyday human problems. You are the reason the High Court of the Coffee Bean exists. You made Cress. You made Mor. You made Dranian. You made Shayne.

Also, I need to thank my husband Phil for telling me to publish my first book back in 2020. Some days I still sit and think about that moment, and I marvel at how much has changed in our lives simply because I had a supportive husband who wanted me to live my dream. I still can't believe how much has happened since that day. I still can't believe I get to do this as my job now.

Thank you to Chase, Ellie, and Austin. To my mom, my dad, my weird siblings, their even weirder spouses, and last but not least, thank you to my nieces and nephews (I'm looking at you, Norah) for reading and loving my books.

Thank you, the reader, for being a part of Dranian's (and Luc's story.)